THE DARK CORNER

THE DARK CORNER UNIVERSE
BOOK 1

DAVID W. ADAMS

CONTENTS

ISBN:
978-1-916582-43-9 [Paperback]
978-1-916582-44-6 [eBook]
978-1-916582-18-7 [Hardcover]

ECHO ON PUBLICATIONS

NOTE FROM THE AUTHOR

Firstly, I would like to thank you for picking up a copy of this revised, reformatted, and brand spanking new version of a *Dark Corner* book. I will never take that for granted and appreciate each and every one of you for doing so.

Let's cut to the chase.

This is not the first version of these books, as some of you may know. However, being an independent author comes with limitations, and for me at least, a great deal of impatience. When I wrote the original *Dark Corner* book, it was in the midst of the Coronavirus Pandemic, and the UK was in its first official lockdown. Go nowhere, do nothing, see nobody.

Basically my life in a nutshell, if you exclude going to work.

But I learned one day in my miserable and bland meandering through the days, that self-publishing had been on the rise while I looked the other way dreaming of having the time and money to be able to potentially have a crack at finally getting all of the stories out of my head. But better than that, was when I discovered there was a way to do it for FREE!

I was warned by several forums and articles that KDP, although an excellent resource compared to the previous nothingness, was also full of issues, pitfalls, and Amazon's usual greedy ways. You will make no money, nobody will see your book if you have less than 50 reviews, and nobody reads horror these days anyway.

Sadly, I must admit, that I was tempted to chuck the briefly stirred ambition of mine in the bin, and carry on going to work everyday during an outbreak so people could buy their 'essential' bathroom paint or Sharpie marker pens.

But it was my wife who encouraged me to continue. She had always written both poetry and fan fictions, but had never felt comfortable with the idea of the world reading her work. She was, however, incredibly persuasive, and after I reworked a story I started writing 20 years previously into what became the first story, *The White Dress*, I got bit by the bug. Over the course of 2020, I wrote ten short stories varying in severity, but overall quite reserved for horror, and resolved to get them published come what may.

Sadly, I couldn't afford an editor or proofreader, and my wife was also working full time and so simply didn't have the time to read for me. And so I decided to publish through a previously unknown, to me at least, website called My Bestseller. They were based in the Netherlands, and required you to buy an ISBN number or publish without one. However, while they offered expanded distribution, this did not include Amazon. I also discovered after purchasing an ISBN for that original version of the book, that it came at a reduced cost for one reason. The code was registered to the website. Which meant exclusivity.

Bollocks.

Exclusivity and not even on Amazon? No this would simply not do. I did however, make it work for a while, and in the course of three months sold a whopping two copies. I bought more than that myself!

Then came the time to explore KDP properly. I had published the book on My Bestseller without ever proofreading or editing it. I figured nobody was going to read it so didn't really worry about it. But one day, when writing the stories for the second book, *Return to the Dark Corner*, I went back to examine plot points that could be expanded.

Shit.

Errors, grammar issues, typos everywhere and more worryingly, plot holes. But it wasn't too late! Barely anybody had read it so I could fix it!

That's when I revised the book, and published through KDP, which came with free ISBNs! Jackpot I thought! But you must remember I was incredibly naïve and undereducated in this area. Exclusivity was a requirement again, but I didn't care. It was Amazon! Everyone uses Amazon! I even got suckered into Kindle Unlimited with the promise of more royalties. They really do know how to con you into things!

Anyway, since then, the *Dark Corner* series has grown and grown, even into producing several pieces of merchandise for the series such as posters and keyrings. The series concludes in the 13th book, a number I chose because I figured it fitting for something that began as a horror series primarily, although it became so much more!

And when the opportunity came along to work with Christian Francis to redesign, reformat and relaunch the series with a new uniform and polished look, I jumped at the chance. Christian put the shine to my stories that I had always hoped to achieve, and even redesigned the covers for me to give it a true 'series' look. I will be forever grateful for his generosity, hard work, and friendship, and am honored for these versions of my works to fall under the banner of Echo On Publishing.

So here we are, entering the *Dark Corner* once again. But I don't do things lightly. These are not simply redesigns of the exact same work. Oh no. My conscience wouldn't allow that! So every single book has an extra short story included to further expand this varied, fascinating and horrific universe. Consider it my gift of thanks to you all for sticking with me, encouraging me not to give up, and pushing me to do better.

As always, I encourage you to be kind, be healthy, and stay safe.
And thank you.

David W. Adams
28th November 2023

*This book is dedicated to
William Henry Griffiths.*

*My grandfather.
My best friend.
I miss you every day.*

THE WHITE DRESS

The library was mostly quiet, just the gentle hum of the computers, and occasional tapping of keyboard keys broke the silence. The secret stares of the middle-aged man in round spectacles, trying to see if anyone was watching him typing *Pornhub* into the address bar. The elderly man on the far left of the row browsing through page after page of Russian Mail Order brides. The haggard looking woman in the middle of the second row struggling to keep her head scarf on and containing her tears whilst looking at the *Dignitas* website. And then there was Sienna.

Occasionally, she would look up from her screen just to ensure her latte takeaway cup was still there, and that the contents were still cold having been ignored for the last three hours. But her gaze was transfixed to article after article containing new information on her latest chosen subject.

This time, the material in question was unexplained deaths believed to be the result of paranormal activity. Sienna liked to completely submerse herself in new topics every so often. She had plenty of time on her hands. The Coronavirus pandemic had seen to that. Six weeks in intensive care on a ventilator, followed by furlough pay, followed by the entire factory closing.

For now, the best she could do was keep her brain active whilst waiting for something to magically appear to solve all her financial problems, and her personal ones. Going to the *Job Centre* every two weeks wasn't exactly expanding her mind's eye.

Last month, she had immersed her brain in learning Portuguese, in the hopes that one day she may get to go on holiday again and being inspired by a new acquaintance. The month before, it was learning everything she could about Black History.

Despite never being what you would call an academic superstar, her brain soaked things up with a sponge. She normally tried to choose something completely random or something she was not remotely interested in. After all, knowledge was power. Well, under normal circumstances. But this time, something had caught her eye and she wanted to know more. Actually, that's not quite true. She wanted to know everything. She needed the distraction.

As the most recent headline came up on the computer monitor, dated four weeks previously, her eyes were transfixed on the artist sketch beneath the banner headline which read, *"Sea claims third victim."* The sketch was of the cliff top over Towan Beach, the sea below, and a figure on the top, dressed in white. The article gave more detail.

"For the third time in as many months, the body of a young woman was washed up in the harbour this morning after what an eyewitness described as a plunge from the clifftops above.

Mr Jonathan Tremblett described the events as he saw them. 'I saw the woman crossing the bridge to the Island, but it looked like she was talking to someone. When I walked further along past the aquarium, I could see there was a young woman, maybe twenty years of age standing on the edge past the main house, wearing a white dress. The lady approached the figure and seemed to fall through her and off the cliff. I watched her hit the waters below, and when I looked back up, the girl in white was gone.'

Similar stories have been making the rounds following the deaths of

local cafe waitress Cheryl Coleman and tourist Natalie Smith.
Devon and Cornwall Police have released a brief statement.

'At 3.05am this morning, the body of a young woman believed to be
that of Miss Christine Charles, was recovered from the water in
Newquay Harbour by a fishing trawler. Police and paramedics were
called to the scene where the victim was pronounced dead and was
then taken by ambulance to hospital. Despite the reported eyewitness
account of Mr Tremblett, there are believed to be no suspicious
circumstances surrounding the death and appears to be yet another
tragic accident. People are reminded that walks along the grounds
surrounding 'The Island' are prohibited unless staying at the home
and are also to be discouraged in violent weather. Miss Charles'
family have been informed.'

We will of course bring you more on this story as things develop."

As Sienna left the library, not by choice, but because they were
closing, she decided to grab a fresh coffee. The appeal of her five-hour
stone cold mocha, no longer appealed to her.

Being after five, all the small cafes she liked to visit were closing and
the big national chains never felt cosy enough. Too impersonal. Too
corporate. *Walkabout* was open, but she wasn't in the mood for rowdy
tourists and sports fans, and so she decided to head home instead, but
not before taking a small detour down to Towan beach.

The wind was building up again, the sun nearly gone from behind
the clouds, and the tide was reaching the base of the Island. Sienna
walked down onto the sand, squelching underfoot not from the
approaching tide, but from the deluge of rain that had fallen just an
hour previously. She looked up at the swaying suspension bridge
between the mainland and the rock containing the house they called
'The Island.'

The house had never appealed to Sienna, too modern, too expensive.
It was the rock formation itself which captured her imagination. In the
previous November, she had decided to focus on developing her artistic
skills and tried to learn several new techniques using *YouTube* tutorials,

and she had always drawn the rock without the house sat atop. Being private land, she'd never been up there, although she was tempted. Her detective tendencies were twinging from all those episodes of *Bones* and *Diagnosis Murder*.

The rocks below, and the tidal pools were now fully consumed by the darkening waters. She took one last look at the top of the cliff edge, and squinting through the returning rain, she swore she could see a faint white glow, but before she could take a second look, a huge bang of thunder rattled the air and she jumped, losing her shoe in the saturated sand. She picked up her shoe, scrambled off the beach, and reached into her bag for her umbrella, fumbling past her phone, which was showing three missed calls from 'Darren'.

As she stumbled through the rain back up to the main part of the town, from the top of the rocks, the girl in white turned, and walked back away from the edge.

"Miss the bus too?"

The voice was almost lost entirely as Sienna was still pawing through her phone for more details on the recent deaths and searching for any correlation in the local area. So far it seemed confined to Newquay.

"Couldn't have missed it by more than five minutes." The voice continued to attempt conversation.

"Here, you look like you could do with this."

The hand that came into Sienna's view was holding a pack of tissues, and the appearance of the hand finally snapped Sienna out of her bubble. As she followed the hand upwards, it was encased in a leather jacket, clearly well worn, and the person wearing it, although no more than twenty-five or so, also seemed to have been well worn.

It was the eyes.

She couldn't put her finger on it, but his eyes were different. Unique. After staring at him for what seemed like five minutes, she realised she hadn't said anything.

"I'm, erm, yes, thank you. Thank you. Sorry, I was just, sorry."

Sienna was never one for socialising, especially with strange men in a thunderstorm. That was a lesson she had recently learned, with harsh consequences. But the man in the bus stop was unfazed, and smiled at her, continuing to hold the tissues out for her to take. As she accepted them, he lowered his arm and introduced himself.

"I'm Jim. I work in the sweet shop behind the bank." "I'm, erm, my, I'm Sienna."

She didn't know what about this man made her want to do it, but she felt compelled to show him what had captured her attention so much. Maybe she felt she owed him an explanation for ignoring his presence for so long.

"I don't have a job right now, so I read about things. I like to learn about new cultures, or history, or in this case, creepy happenings."

She turned her phone to show Jim an article from *The Sun* about the second death, four weeks prior. Jim looked at the picture of Natalie Smith, and his smile faded slightly.

"I knew her. She came into the shop a few times while she was staying here. We'd arranged to meet up for a coffee, but she never showed. Then this happened."

Sienna felt like she had stabbed Jim with a dagger as he turned away from her, and his smile seemed to turn to a look of regret.

"I'm so sorry, I didn't mean to upset you. I've just been reading about the deaths. Something seems unnatural about them."

She turned back to her phone and scrolled along to the report of Cheryl Coleman's death the month before Natalie's, and Jim looked back towards the screen.

"I knew her too."

He said it with more sadness than he had with Natalie, like there was deeper meaning for this loss.

"We were together for three months. I was heading to work one day, and I walked into her and knocked her lunch out of her hands. She shouted and bawled at me and called me every name under the sun, but I just stared at her like she was perfect. I kept popping by the cafe where she worked, annoying her, making silly jokes, bringing her lunch, until eventually she decided to go on a date with me. We were due to go away for the weekend, the day she died."

Sienna felt awful. This nice man had sat next to her, offered her a tissue, and tried to make conversation whilst waiting for the bus, and she had just brought back all the misery he had suffered in the last three months.

"I'm sorry. If I'd have known, I would have been less thoughtless. I don't tend to make much conversation. The last time I talked to a stranger, it didn't work out well."

Jim looked at her and smiled.

"That's okay, it's a small town, at some point you kinda get that everybody knows everybody else."

Sienna felt comforted by that thought, although she had lived here in Newquay for three years, and she'd never seen Jim before. Then again, she didn't get out much unless it was heading to the Job centre or to the library.

"Hey," Jim said. "The next bus isn't for an hour, did you maybe wanna grab a coffee from *McDonalds* or something? I'd suggest a little cafe I know, but they're all closed now."

Knowing she was cold, and probably on the verge of hypothermia, Sienna glanced at the live timetable, and agreed.

McDonalds was an eatery of two halves this night. One half was taken up by the rowdy youths, finished school for the day, pretending they were ten years older than they were, swearing, wearing clothes way too inappropriate for their age, and the other half was pretty much empty apart from a lone businessman, working on his laptop, clearly having been there a while judging by the six latte cups that surrounded him, tie skewed to one side and a look of emptiness in his eyes.

Jim started the conversation back up by targeting the topic of death.

"So, are you fascinated by death this month, or just ghosts?"

Sienna looked a little surprised at his statement given the subject matter of their meeting just twenty minutes ago but relished any chance to talk about her latest fixation.

"I saw the news when the first victim died, but then I noticed that this had happened before, so I started doing a little research, and I discovered that every eighteen years, there have been four deaths in four consecutive months from that rock formation."

For a brief moment, she recalled how Jim said he was close to two of the dead women, and although caution began creeping into her mind, she dismissed it with another glance into those eyes. She decided to continue.

"The earliest report of it that I could find was in eighteen-forty- two, when an eighteen-year-old woman threw herself off the cliff after finding out her lover had betrayed her with her sister and three others. Some say they saw her lover on the clifftop with her, but he denied it. He was so distraught following her death, that he poisoned himself three days later in the hope of being reunited with her in the afterlife. The sister who he had cheated with was the second victim, four weeks later."

Jim looked deeply interested. "And the third victim?"

Sienna was getting into her rhythm now. "The third death that year was the month after the sister, when a member of a wealthy family living near Fistral, claimed to see her maid arguing with her husband in the gardens of the house, before storming out of the grounds. The next morning, they found her body dashed on the bottom of the cliff, the local police reporting sightings of a woman in white talking to her moments before. The husband was investigated as the main suspect, and being the patriarch of a wealthy family, sleeping with the hired help caused quite a scandal, but no formal charges were ever brought."

"You said there were four every time?"

Jim seemed focused like a laser beam, really getting into the narrative.

"You'd never believe me if I told you who the fourth victim was," replied Sienna.

A wry smile crept across her face, but Jim's was craving more story.

"You see, the wealthy wife had a sister." Jim smiled.

"He didn't?" Sienna smiled back.

"Oh, he did. And the maid caught him, on the bed she had just changed. A month after the maid leapt to her death, the wealthy woman's sister washed up in the harbour, after the husband had chased her through the streets. He'd watched her cross the bridge to the cliff and claimed a woman in white pushed her over the edge. Trouble was, when *he* reached the cliff edge, there was nobody there."

"And that was it?"

Jim seemed mildly disappointed.

"Seems a bit random, four deaths in four months, and then nothing for eighteen years."

"People have speculated that the deaths occur every eighteen years because the original woman was eighteen when she died, and there are four deaths because the lover cheated with four women. Supernatural happenings tend to develop into conspiracy theories."

Sienna looked around and most of the people had left. The place was quiet, other than the background beeping of the fryers, and the printing of receipts.

Jim moved his coffee cup out of the way and leaned in some more.

"And this happens every eighteen years, right?" Sienna nodded.

"And is there any correlation between these women, and is it always women?"

Sienna flicked through pages on her phone, but she couldn't see any reports of male deaths, or links between families.

"None that I can see, and no male victims, but always that spot. Even since the house was built on top, the place of jumping is always the same. You'd think it would put people off staying there."

Jim chuckled.

"Not judging by the prices!"

The two of them shared a laugh for a few moments, before Sienna glanced at the time.

"Oh shit! We've been here two hours! The last bus has gone!"

She grabbed her coat and bag and started to head for the door. Her phone vibrated to the sound of an incoming call, but she didn't notice. The rain had calmed to a mild drizzle now, but the bus was long gone, and the taxi rank was empty. Jim stood up to follow her, seemingly undisturbed by this turn of events.

"Sorry, I was a little caught up in the story, I didn't notice either. We could call for a taxi, but being Friday night, we may have a wait on our hands."

Jim zipped up his jacket and placed his hands in his pockets. Sienna's phone vibrated again, this time she noticed. The screen read '**Darren calling**'. She sighed, shouted "not now!" and shoved the phone back in her bag. She looked back at Jim and turned back to face him.

"I'm sorry, I tend to get a little uncomfortable when I break out of my routine. I did that recently and it caused nothing but trouble. I'm usually home by now."

Her phone vibrated again, this time to alert Sienna to a voicemail, but she swiped it off the screen, and sat back down at the table. Jim joined her and put his hand on her shoulder.

"It's okay, it's probably my youthful good looks and winning enthusiasm that threw you off kilter."

He smiled, fishing for one to be returned. It worked. Sienna giggled and agreed, that he had somewhat made her forget her routine.

"We could get another coffee while we wait for that taxi if you like, or we could take a walk?"

Sienna looked at Jim, and then looked outside. The drizzle made its way slowly down the glass, and yet the night air looked inviting.

"A walk would be nice."

The stroll through the town was quiet, and it was almost like it was just the two of them. A few revellers spilled out of *Walkabout* shouting something about how *United* were robbed and 'no way was that a fucking penalty' but as the rain cleared, and the moon became visible, everything seemed so serene.

The only slight annoyance was the constant vibrating of Sienna's phone in her bag. The missed call count had now reached ten, and three text messages, but she was too into the moment to take any notice. Whatever stress awaited on the other end of that phone could wait. She'd put it off for this long, a little longer wouldn't matter.

After a while, she noticed Jim was steering her down towards Towan beach, and the images of articles and death reports came flooding back into her mind, but when she began to hear the crashing of the waves, the sounds drowned everything out.

Whether harsh weather or calm, the sound of the ocean hitting the beach or the rocks, or even gently lapping at the sand, was so relaxing it could lull even the harshest of people into contentment. The closer they got, the less Sienna noticed the vibration of her phone, and the more she held on to Jim's arm. She felt so close to him, and yet she had only known him a few hours. She wondered if he understood the trust he engendered.

As they walked up to the wall overlooking the beach, they stopped, and stared at the moonlight over the cliff top.

"Beautiful, isn't it," asked Jim, transfixed to the sky. "I love coming here at night. Everything is so perfect. The moonlight is so clear."

And then a shift in his vocal tone. "Nothing escapes the moonlight."

Sienna missed the voice change and remained in her own little world.

"I don't stay out much after dark, but I have to admit, I could stand here all night."

She followed the shadows of the waves on the rocks, and the mist like body of the clouds moving across the face of the moon.

And then she saw her.

Standing on the bridge between the mainland and the Island, was the figure in the white dress. Sienna felt a chill run through her body, as the woman stared directly at her. She moved her hand down to meet Jim's and the cold touch of his skin made her jump.

"What is it?" he asked, gripping her hand tightly.

With no change in Sienna's face, he followed her gaze up to the bridge. She finally found her words.

"She's there."

Jim looked at the bridge, and then back at Sienna. "We should follow her," he said.

"Are you fucking serious?" Sienna blasted him with her words, a look of disbelief at his statement.

"Do you wanna find out what's going on or not? Someone could be in trouble. You've read the stories; people think this woman lures people over the edge like some kind of siren.

Don't you wanna know if she's real?"

Jim let go of Sienna's hand and began running towards the stone stairs which led to the top of the mainland.

"Jim, what are you doing?"

Sienna called after him. He didn't reply and kept climbing the stairs, and before long was out of sight. She looked back at the bridge and the figure had turned to one side. Her feet seemed to be a good three or four inches off the surface of the bridge, almost like she was floating. As it moved in the wind, she remained still.

Then Sienna saw what she was looking at. Jim had appeared at the entrance to the bridge. Frozen in place, Sienna watched the figure turn around and move along the bridge, gliding through the air, not touching the bridge or the rails on either side. Jim moved slowly behind her, focused on her image, also not touching the rails.

Sienna called to him, and the figure in white turned to face her slightly, before continuing towards the cliff edge, moving past the house. Jim reached the other side of the bridge before Sienna found it in herself to move out of her statue like existence. She ran for the stone steps, climbing them as fast as she could. Her foot slipped as she reached the top and her bag fell onto the ground, spilling her phone onto the grass. She picked up the phone and ran towards the bridge. She could see neither Jim nor the figure. The rain began to splash her face as the clouds moved back in towards the moon.

As she made her way across the swaying bridge, her phone began to vibrate. '*Darren calling*' appeared on the screen yet again. She ignored the call and reached the other side of the bridge. As she ran past the house, through the gardens, her phone rang again. This time out of sheer frustration, she answered the phone.

"Not now Darren! I don't have time for this, I'm trying to save someone's life!"

As she uttered the words, she stopped dead, holding the phone to her ear.

"Hello? Sienna? Are you there? We need to talk about this. Hello? Talk to me! You can't just leave me for him!"

The voice down the phone became irater, but Sienna was locked onto the image of the figure in white standing on the edge of the cliff, and Jim standing next to her.

They fixed their gaze on each other, and the white woman beckoned Jim closer. Sienna dropped the phone on the grass and ran for Jim. The voice was still shouting out of the phone, but became more distant as Sienna bolted towards Jim, hands outstretched.

She was within six feet of him when he reached out for the woman in the white dress. He moved through her, and his body tumbled over the edge like a domino and the figure stepped back. Sienna was too much in motion to stop herself. She reached out her hand and slid onto her front, sliding across the wet grass to catch his hand, but it was too late.

Sienna slid past the white figure, looking into her empty black eyes, and off the edge of the cliff. As her body fell through the wind and rain, she turned back to face the top of the cliff she had just left and saw Jim standing next to the woman in white, holding her hand. And as they moved back from the edge of the cliff, Sienna plunged into the eternal darkness of the ocean below.

EIGHTEEN YEARS LATER

"So, what brings you to Newquay?" the interviewer asked.

Sarah didn't really have a planned answer for this. She had spent the weekend preparing for all questions relating to finance, admin, filing, but she hadn't counted on small talk.

"Well, I lived here a long time ago, but I had a messy breakup, and decided to make a clean break."

The interviewer seemed intrigued and pressed for more.

"I don't really want to go into the details, it's rather personal. Let's just say I made a mistake with someone and thought running away would solve it. But I guess it didn't. I have family here, and I've had a tough time of it lately, so decided now was the time to come home."

"Okay, well thank you for sharing, the interview went great, and we'll be in touch."

Reading the rejection letter for the third time didn't make it any better, but Sarah was becoming familiar with the feeling of failure. She'd felt it before, six years ago when she ran from here. She closed her email app and opened the latest news on the Devon Live app. She began reading about the anniversary of somebody's death but wasn't really taking in the words.

Her concentration slipped and she dropped the phone off the table and knocked her coffee over at the same time. As she sunk her head in her hands, she saw her phone appear back on the table, intact and still open to the article.

"I think you dropped this."

A man's voice caused her to raise her head from her hands. A man in a leather jacket was standing over her, smiling, pointing to her phone.

"Reading anything interesting?" he asked.

Sarah glanced at the phone and summarised the article.

"Not really. Tonight, is the anniversary of some woman's death and they're wondering if there's gonna be another."

The man sat down opposite Sarah and pressed for more. "How did she die?"

Sarah, not sure why she was talking to this man, pulled more information from the article.

"Erm... she jumped off the cliffs on Towan Beach where the 'Island' house used to be. There were four deaths in four months. All women, all jumped from the same spot. Seems like they were all cheaters."

Sarah sighed heavily.

"Something I'm familiar with. Maybe I'll be next." The man smiled and reached a hand across the table. "Hi. I'm Jim."

BOUND BY PAIN

Driving at night really was the worst thing in the world. The glare of the oncoming traffic, the complete blindness of driving rain combined with headlights and the constant stabbing of the white lines.

Alex had never liked driving in the dark. In the early mornings, he was too tired, in the late evenings he was fed up and tired.

Driving for work was even worse. He was stuck in that awful never space between apprentice and executive. Too successful to take the train, but not successful enough for the private jet. And all to secure a yearlong extension to a sponsorship deal for seats at a third rate stadium.

Alex used to thirst for adventure, or at least some kind of interesting event to occur every so often, but now, even that would seem too much effort. The rain began picking up even more, and the wipers were on the verge of flying off the windscreen, they were going that fast. The car hit a pothole, and the *Monster* energy drink that was sat in the cup holder flew up and tipped all over the passenger seat.

"God damn it!" shouted Alex.

He began reaching into the back to grab a tissue or cloth of some sort.

"I could have spilled bottled water, but no, I had to choose the fluorescent nuclear shit."

Alex had only had his company car for three weeks, and already he'd dropped a handful of fries down the side of the driver's seat, lost half a *Krispy Kreme* somewhere under the passenger seat, and now there was an increasingly bright yellow stain forming on the cream carpet.

"Cream. Who in their right mind decided to design a carpet for a car and went with cream. Cars have floor mats for a reason, and they're always black for a reason!"

Keeping an eye on the road and trying to clean up energy drink was proving quite a challenge. As the car drifted into the oncoming lane, the obligatory honk from an oncoming vehicle snapped Alex back to attention. This time, Alex lost his bag of *Doritos* into the toxic puddle which began to form a three-mile island of orange evil, bubbling away into the fibres of the floor.

Leaning over again, the car began to drift towards the other side of the road once again, but this time, the movement went unnoticed. As Alex retrieved the empty bag from the floor, dripping in cheese flavoured slop, the deafening roar of a truck horn shattered the silence of the cabin. Alex looked up to see nothing but light barrelling towards him, and much like a deer, for a moment, was caught in the glare. The horn sounded once again, and Alex yanked the wheel to the side. The car lurched painfully to one side, catching a river of rainwater with the front wheels, sending the car spinning three-sixty, facing the back of the narrowly avoided truck. The eighteen-wheeler was still honking as it drove away, and Alex's car veered round again until it was pointed in the right direction once more.

Alex gripped the steering wheel, the car now steady, travelling at a very ordinary forty miles per hour, eyes focussed on the road ahead. He could hear his own heart thumping in his ears.

He looked in the rear-view mirror to see the disappearing taillights of the truck moving around the corner... and a pair of eyes looking back at him from the back seat. Alex snapped his head around to see the figure of a man sat on the back seat.

"Well, that was certainly close, wasn't it?"

Alex snapped his head back around, slammed on the brake pedal, and yanked the wheel out of fear, sending the car lumbering to one side. It caught the edge of the road, and the back bounced up. The car lifted into the air, barrel rolling across the tarmac, the sound of metal twisting, glass breaking, the tiny fragments bouncing along the road. The carcass of the car smashed through the fence on the other side of the road, roof first, and bounced down the bank, hitting several trees in the process. The mud flung up from the ground as if explosions had detonated from hidden mines.

As the car slowed, and made its final roll, the rear tyres departed the shell and carried on into the darkness, and the vehicle came to rest on its roof, creaking like a slain monster emitting its final breath.

The smell of fuel was the first thing Alex sensed as he returned to the land of the living. The pain shooting through his head was as if someone had driven an ice pick into his brain. His vision was incredibly blurred, and the stinging in his temple was accompanied by the gradual trickle of blood. As incredible as the incident had been, the first thing to enter his mind was how he might be able to clean cheese flavouring out of the carpet, but blood was never coming out.

The driver side door was jammed shut, or at least what was left of it. Alex managed to unclip his seatbelt and propped his arms up against the roof which was now only about a foot from his face. He gradually manoeuvred his torso over the gear stick, when he felt an intense pain shoot through his right leg.

"Ah fuck! Jesus Christ!"

He relaxed his leg, and a shaft of light pierced the woodlands to expose a very dark wet patch on his trousers. He suspected something was broken, but from the increasing strength of the fuel smell, he knew he had to get out of there. He grabbed the edge of the now smashed window in the passenger door. Small fragments of glass that hadn't been shaken out of the frame pierced his fingers as he pulled his broken body through and landed in a bog of mud and broken branches. After screaming out in pain once more, Alex began to pull himself along the ground, using some of the larger sticks as anchors in the mud.

He settled a short distance away from the wreckage and pulled himself up onto a smooth rock. His phone was still in his pocket. As he pulled it out, of course the screen was smashed, but the time was still just visible. He activated the torch to get a better look at his surroundings. The car had travelled a long way from the road. In this darkness and with the rain that had fallen, nobody would find him until daylight.

He glanced at the time again. ***00.09*** He angled the torch on the phone down to his leg, rolling up the trousers carefully to find that the wound was in fact a very large gash, but as he tested his weight on it, he was relieved to see it wasn't broken. He looked back at the shattered phone screen.

"Typical. Of course, there's no service. Why would there be? I'm in a horror movie."

Alex mumbled profanities to himself as he sat back on the rock, leaning up against the neighbouring tree. He closed his eyes for a moment.

"You know, you're a terrible driver."

The voice snapped Alex to maximum alertness levels. "What *will* your boss say?"

The figure which had caused the accident in the first place, was now stood directly opposite Alex, leaning nonchalantly against another tree. He was about six-two, around forty-five years of age, and seemed to have a wisp of silvery hair to the left of his head. Alex couldn't tell whether the silvery effect was caused by the emerging moonlight but decided to focus on how its owner was even present.

"Who the fuck are you?"

Alex's tone was breathy, revealing that apparently, he was not quite the picture of perfect health he thought he was.

"I think the better question is, *what* am I?" replied the stranger.

Alex reached around for some kind of weapon, or piece of wreckage, never moving his eyes from the figure.

"Alex, you can't hurt me. I would've thought our little tumble down the hill had proved that."

"So, what, you're some kind of superhero? A God perhaps? Or are you my guardian angel?"

Whatever Alex was now facing, sarcasm was his only remaining weapon. The figure stood upright and moved towards him in a rather jolly manner, a spring in his step, and as he moved into the full shaft of moonlight, Alex was surprised to see a very familiar, and yet impossible face.

"Q?" asked Alex.

Completely confused, Alex was now staring at the actor John deLancie, in full *Starfleet* uniform, as the character Q from *Star Trek The Next Generation*.

Smiling, the man responded.

"No, Alex. I'm not Q, nor the actor who portrays him. I have simply taken the form of someone I knew you would recognise. Someone who would get a reaction from you."

Completely convinced he was now hallucinating, Alex took a moment, and then responded.

"Okay so now what? Is Captain Picard going to beam me up to the *Enterprise* and reveal my life has been nothing but a dream? What exactly *are* you?"

Q smiled and moved to sit on the rock next to Alex, putting him on edge.

"Oh, I've been many things over the centuries. I've been a maid, a nurse, a jolly old policeman. I was even a President once. That was fun."

His eyes narrowed and he leaned his face closer to Alex.

"I've also been a vampire. And a werewolf. And a demon. Hell, tormenting ghost hunters is a hugely satisfying activity in my spare time. I've had Zak Bagans running around after me so many times, he should have an Olympic Gold medal by now!"

Alex felt the side of his head, as a jolt of pain reminded him of his situation.

"Ah yes, you're injuries. Well what good is it to look like Q if I don't act like him?"

The man snapped his fingers and with a flash of light, Alex was completely back to his normal self. No pain, no blood, even his clothes were clean and pressed. He stood to his feet quickly and moved a couple of feet further away from the apparently god-like entity. He turned back to face him.

"You're welcome. Now maybe you'll listen to me."

"It's erm, a little off-putting watching a fictional character come to life and fix you up. I'm still not sure I'm awake."

Clearly angered by the lack of sincerity coming from Alex, Q stood up, marched towards him, anger taking over his expression, and his form began to twist and contort. Alex staggered back in fear, as the man who was previously human shaped had now grown to around ten feet, and now resembled the image of the Devil.

Horns sprouted from his head, and a tail lashed out behind him. He reached down and grabbed Alex by the throat, lifting him up from the ground. He brought him close to his face, the stench of death billowing from the mouth, Alex grasping at the muscled forearms gripped around his throat, legs dangling in the air. The demon turned Alex towards the wreck of his company car, still sat on its roof, a small fire now forming around the fuel tank.

"That is where you should still be now!" bellowed the creature. "If you want to go back there, I can arrange it, but don't trifle with me. I've dealt with millions of souls across the centuries, and you are not so significant to stand above any of those. So, I suggest you listen to me *very* carefully."

With another flash of light, Alex crumpled to the floor, choking on air, and was once again in the presence of the *Star Trek* fan favourite.

"Now, I believe I have your attention."

"What… what is it you want from me?" Alex asked through garbled breaths and squinting through forced tears. "And where… where did you come from?"

Satisfied that he had the full attention of Alex, Q explained his purpose.

"It's funny really, how life only starts when you die. Believe me, I know. I was like you once. Well, a very long time ago. I was a young porter at a medical facility in Iowa. I was assisting a brilliant young doctor attempting to stop gangrene from claiming the leg of the local blacksmith. I remember handing the doctor a clean bandage, and then… nothing."

Alex looked confused, so Q continued.

"You see, the blacksmith owed money to a villainous creature named Goldsmith. He'd lost trade because he couldn't stand in the workshop all day and had not made the payment on his loan, so Mr Goldsmith decided to express his… displeasure.

Only I got in the way. The next morning, I woke up in bed, next to a beautiful woman. My wife, apparently, although I still had memories of working in the surgery and appeared to have aged ten years. Gradually, my life came into focus, and I got used to being inside the body of someone else, in a different country, in a different life. Paris was beautiful eight hundred years ago by the way.

Anyway, I lived a long life, raised three children, all girls, all as beautiful as their mother, right through into adulthood. And then I lost them. My wife, Cherie, was coveted by another man. He attempted to woo her away from me. She refused, so he killed her. Slit her throat from ear to ear. Then he did the same to my three girls. I found him standing over the naked body of my eldest daughter holding the knife, covered in her blood. I just stood there. And as I felt the knife plunge into my heart, I was already seeing myself standing in front of a mirror, a lifetime away.

I became an artist in my next life. But I always felt out of place, still retaining the memories of the horrors that had gone before. I couldn't understand how this was happening to me. It wasn't reincarnation, I was moving into existing bodies in different time periods, and whoever was in those bodies previously, was gone forever."

Alex was entirely captivated by this story, even as behind him, the entire car began to catch fire. He posed a question.

"So how did you learn what was happening to you? Clearly you are some kind of supernatural being?"

Q smiled and nodded.

"It took me four hundred years to finally learn what I was. I wasn't actually dead. My first memory died the moment Mr Goldsmith swung his axe, but I wasn't. I existed for a purpose. You see Alex, every time I have died, it has been in an unjust, or violent manner. I've lived six hundred lives, and not once did I die peacefully in my sleep, or from natural causes.

Always painful. Surely there was a reason for this happening to me, not only to die repeatedly, but to retain the memories of every lifetime, and suffer as heavily as I did. And then I met someone. Someone like me. I had been placed in the body of a vampire."

Alex raised his eyebrows with both intrigue, and a look of concern on his face. Q responded.

"Yes, Alex, monsters are real, and no, they don't twinkle in sunlight. They burn."

"Well, I had to ask," Alex replied.

"Yes, I'm sure. Anyway, this other person found me living in Plymouth in England at the time, mid-nineteenth century, working in the market every day on a fruit stall. I was sixteen years old, and one day a beautiful woman approached me as I was sweeping up around the stall. She bent over in front of me and stared deep into my eyes. She ran her hands over my face and down my chest. I'll never forget what she said to me.

'I wonder how many lives you've lived. I guess one more won't hurt.'

She pulled out two knives, ran one through my heart, and the other through her own. But this time was different. Instead of moving straight into another body, I floated above my current one, and found myself stood next to the woman on a balcony of a neighbouring building. The woman turned to me and took my hand. She walked me in silence, through the building, nobody inside even noticing our presence. She said nothing until we moved down the stairs and out into the street. There was a commotion over the double death inside the market. I looked through the entrance and saw the two bodies, eyes wide open, blood mingling on the floor between the two of us. The woman stopped. She turned to me and spoke.

'Your time has come my young friend. You've served your purpose and taken on your suffering with pride. But we have other plans for you now.'

Needless to say, I was intrigued."

Alex craved more information, the car now fully aflame, the heat radiating on his skin. Never had he been so engrossed in a tale. For now, he suspended reality, ignored the fact he was talking to a demon, or a ghost, or whatever he was. Even ignoring the fact that vampires were real. Something was drawing him in to every word the being was saying.

"I need to know the rest," he said.

"Indeed, my friend, I owe you the full truth. After all, we can't make use of you if you don't know everything."

Alex flinched at the phrase 'make use of you' but was too invested in the story and urged Q to continue.

"She explained to me that I was a pain wraith. I was born in an ethereal form to learn suffering and agony, and misery, and violence. My sole purpose to this point had been to experience different levels of horror. And eventually, when the wraith suffers enough, they are rewarded by moving to the next phase of their existence using the energy gained from their lifetimes of suffering to become... more. Suddenly, I could do things, I'd only ever read about in books. I still moved from body to body for a time, but with the abilities to manipulate reality, albeit in small doses, such as fixing your injuries.

I found I could choose which body to inhabit next, sometimes three or four a decade, without the need for death. My reward for my suffering was complete and total freedom. The woman became my guide, helping me move between bodies, and forms, eventually moving into supernatural forms, inhabiting homes as a spirit, stalking the woodlands of Scotland as a werewolf, experiencing life as never before!

But there was a price for my developing powers. I encountered an individual who was very down on his luck. I was inhabiting his work friend who had been very successful, and he was at risk of losing his home, and his family. I remembered what it was like to lose everything, I had done it many times before.

So, I broke the rules. I used my powers to manipulate the lottery draw that week to match the numbers he had chosen to play every week for twenty years without ever winning even a base prize. He won the jackpot, secured his future, and his families future, and lived happily ever after. But I'd taken one

liberty too far. I'd interfered with the timeline and overstepped the mark. I was ripped from my body and banished back to the ethereal realm I inhabited at my birth. I was subjected to all the pain and suffering I had lived through in my first six hundred years over and over again until I felt the very fabric of my existence being torn apart at the seams.

And then the pain stopped, and I was given another chance. I would work my penance. I would go back to Earth, and keep my abilities, even enhanced, but on one condition. I had to correct the mistakes I made or be subjected to a never-ending lifetime of chained suffering for the rest of time."

As the faint sound of sirens pierced the night sky, and a small explosion rumbled the ground nearby, Alex shed a single tear.

"All for fixing the lottery so a man could keep his home and family. Beings so powerful, and all because of something so trivial, you endured so much suffering?"

Q looked regretful and wistful. The eyes exposing the incredible age of the being within the facade of the fictional character momentarily tearing up. He continued.

"Amazing, isn't it? Six hundred years of life, powers beyond the dreams of the wildest imagination, foiled by one random act of kindness."

"Did you fix the mistake you made?" asked Alex.

Q hesitated for a moment, looked at the ground, and with a wry smile spreading across his face, looked back up at Alex.

"Almost."

Q stood up and moved towards Alex, much more menacing as he had been acting just a moment ago.

"You see, Alex, when I helped my good friend John win the lottery, he bought a very large house with the money, and in that house, he started up a small company. After a couple of years, the company made enough money to purchase a small sports team. That team then employed six people to run marketing and administration, things like that."

Alex began moving back towards the burning wreckage of the car, sirens getting louder as they got closer. Q continuing to advance towards him, taking larger strides. He began to feel an inevitability to the end of this story and his interest began to wane, but not enough that he didn't ask the next question.

"What has this got to do with me?"

The question came out in a whimper, which seemed to excite Q.

"Well, my dear boy, if the lottery prize had not been won, your job would never have existed. You should actually have died the same day John won his prize in a rather nasty car accident. Not surprising given your driving abilities. I silenced John's wife first. She reminded me of my third wife. So beautiful, but had I not interfered in the first place, she had been destined to take her own life. I simply put things right. Then of course, there were the children. Having lost several myself, I knew the least painful way to dispatch them. Next came my old friend. He was due to have thrown himself from the Golden Gate Bridge before I mixed up the numbers, so naturally, I just gave him a hand over the side."

Alex's face was now contorted with terror. The flames of the car now burning at his skin, just feet away, sirens louder than they'd been, they couldn't have been more than a mile from him now.

"I can do a lot, you see, but I can't turn back time. I had to put society back, life back, and take away what shouldn't have been. I'd do anything to stay out of that place, I couldn't bear to suffer that fate for all eternity. So, I removed the fruits of my labour, working my way through the company, burning down the house, eliminating the employees who should never have been on this path. I even got to snack on a few as a vampire.

I'd forgotten how freeing that form could be. I got a little creative with a few of the deaths. Their pre-determined fates were so dull and boring, I thought why not have a little fun?"

Alex's arm began to blister, he was that close to the flames. He could see blue and red lights shimmering nearby.

"You see Alex, you've wasted your life. A life that should have ended years ago. We know, we see what has changed, even if we cannot go back and alter it. You require purpose, and I still have work to do. And you're going to help me. Well, your body is. I'm afraid it's not going to be pleasant"

Q rushed forward, and plunged his fist straight through Alex's chest, the sound of crunching ribs filling the air, so close to the fire, sounding like kindling popping beneath the flames. He gripped Alex's heart in his hand, blood dripping from the cavity, a smile growing wider on his face. Alex's screams were drowned out by the sound of the sirens, now in position at the top of the hill. Q leaned in a little closer, the glow of the flames dancing on his skin, his eyes black as the night.

"As I said before, the people who were in the bodies before me, just vanished, so I guess this is goodbye. Besides with your driving, you'd have killed someone either way."

With one swift squeeze, Q crushed Alex's heart, the scream

shattering the woodlands, causing the police officers to stop in their tracks halfway down the hill.

"What the fuck was that?" remarked one officer.

"I dunno, but we better hurry. Judging from that fire, he could be burning alive down there."

Ten officers in total scrambled down the hillside, following the tracks of the wreckage until they reached the bottom. They came across the burning wreckage just as another explosion rocked the ground. They fell back onto the ground, before clambering back up.

One officer called for the fire department to get down as soon as possible, the sound of more sirens filling the night sky. As one officer moved past a discarded tyre, he spotted a large patch of ground, which seemed to be slick with something dark. He knelt and pressed his finger to the liquid. Focusing his torch on the substance, he saw that it was blood. And it was still warm.

He stood upright and followed a trail in the leaves and branches. Another officer followed him, shining the torch on the ground. Suddenly, the torch revealed a foot, no shoe, and as the torch moved up the leg, and the torso, it met a face beaming back at them.

"Officers, thank goodness you're here. I was rather worried for a minute there."

DOLLY MIXTURES

The house sort of loomed up from the ground, like some great massive plinth. It almost looked like it had come from the Earth itself, its basement windows barely visible buried within the golden-brown leaves, piled in front of the trees they had fallen from.

Vines, and ivy crept their way up the walls like veins, the leaves scratching the weathered windows like fingernails. Even the brickwork was mottled with age, moss on the four corners, tainting the faded red colour with deepest green. The obligatory triangular roof for houses as creepy as this stuck out into the sky like a knife, complete with odd-shaped window, behind which, only darkness was visible. And of course, the faint grey of spiderwebs in the corners.

I hate spiderwebs. I always have. It's not even because they are home to the most hated small creature in the world. It's just how they catch you off guard when you walk through one in the dark and have that total panic that a tarantula is about to eat your face. I knew that a house as ancient as this was bound to be full of them. I had a picture in my head that at some point one evening when watching the TV, it would play out a scene from *Arachnophobia* and spiders would just emerge from every crevice and corner.

Having said that, I'd chosen to buy the house, so deep down, I knew that there would be a reason for it being so cheap. Billed as a 'bit of a fixer upper' is usually how these things go at auction, but that was a bit of an understatement in the case of 1701 Pike Road.

I wasn't much of a handy woman, but I could nail a board down and splash a bit of paint on some walls. However, for this job, I'd have to be more dynamic with my ambitions. *YouTube* was going to come in very handy here. I remember thinking that I wasn't sure if this place even had internet capability. It seemed to pre-date dial up around here let alone the prospect of fibre optics. I'd have to work hard though if I wanted to turn a profit on this place. Maybe I should give you a little back story, you know, like a good narrator…

I'd spent most of my childhood trying to figure out what I wanted to do when I grew up, and most of my early adult life trying to answer the same question. Did I really have to grow up, and why couldn't I just party until I made one of the fatal mistakes like going home with some guy from a club, finding out I'm pregnant, and spending the rest of my life owning the single mother look.

Unfortunately, that decision was taken from me when I lost my parents. Plausible deniability is a wonderful phrase, provided it isn't used against you to get out of paying you compensation. The company responsible for their deaths knew what they had done to cause it, but because there was no record of any abnormalities found in their new car, and no trace of exactly who had failed to notice during production, they got off scot- free.

Eventually of course, being the twenty-first century, they went bankrupt because as we know, no company founded after 2010 can survive for more than ten years without going under. Yet another home-grown car manufacturer vanished from the public eye. When the insurance money finally came through, I'd already managed to alienate most of my friends, dealing with the lawsuit, and even my exes weren't interested.

I didn't have a job, I'd given that up too, but I had a moderate amount of cash to splash. Watching daytime TV gave me the idea to invest in property. It was a case of me needing to occupy my time learning a new skill to gain some kind of interest from anyone, friends, boyfriends, girlfriends, I really didn't care as long as it was attention. And also, to try and gain a bigger return so I didn't end up spaffing all the money up the wall and being right back where I started. I found this house on an auction website, and it piqued my interest because of the *Star Trek* sounding name.

I mean 1701 Pike Road? Seriously? How is any *Trek* fan meant to turn that opportunity down? I researched the history of the place, and it was grim. I mean properly grim. You know how most creepy looking ancient houses look like you'd get murdered there? Well in this one, people actually did. Although when I say people, I mean kids.

In 1807, the first owner of the house, but not the architect I should add, moved into the house with his five children. Over the first five days of the house being inhabited, all five children had died. Or at least, they'd disappeared. The father was seen pacing backwards and forwards in the window of the front room by the neighbours, all day, every day, and every day he would be holding a new doll. At the end of each day, he would place the next doll on the windowsill, to look out at the people passing by.

On the sixth day, he shot himself on the front lawn. Just walked out of the house, knelt on the grass, and pulled the trigger.

Witness statements from the time, recorded the sight of the dolls turning their heads towards the man, just before he pulled the trigger. Then boom, splat, strawberry jam all over the place. The children were never found, and the dolls and all the other possessions of the family were taken up to the attic and stored until the next family came along.

The house lay empty until 1823. 31st October they moved in. I know right? Why would you move into a murder house on Halloween. I couldn't make this shit up. A woman and her husband moved in, this time with three children. The very first night, a group of trick or treaters knocked on the front door and got no reply. When one of the kids tried the door handle, the door swung open, and what they say traumatised them for life. The mum and dad were hanging from the banister over the stairwell, and three dolls were sat on the stairs below. No kids in the house. Eight kids missing, eight dolls. Creepy right?

Fast forward to the next family, moving in towards the latter half of 1850. The house had been used on and off by a local coven who were trying to practice their craft out of sight of the whole 'burn the witch' brigade, but when a god-fearing priest tried to burn the house down with them inside, it was boarded up and ear marked for demolition. When that didn't happen, a British Doctor looking for inspiration to write his first novel to keep him busy during his retirement, bought the house, and hired an out-of-town team to renovate the house back to its former glory. Think he was from some place called Newquay. Anyway, I digress.

By this point, a dark cloud hung over this house, but the British man didn't care for that, as far as he was concerned, it was potential story material. One night, the contractors were locking up the house for the night, when they heard crying coming from the attic. Confused as to what the noise was, they made their way up there. They found the British man, sat in the corner, surrounded by dolls, clutching one in his arms, crying and rocking back and forth. When he noticed the men standing in the doorway, he looked up and spoke quite proudly.

"They're so beautiful. Aren't they beautiful! My children!"

One of the workmen claims that the doll the British man was holding, then turned its head towards them and they saw blood dripping from its mouth. They ran out of the house as fast as they could and never returned. And the British man? Nobody ever saw him again. But a new doll appeared in the attic the next time somebody ventured in there.

I know what you're thinking. Why on earth would a single, young woman want to buy a house that she knew was the site of numerous deaths, potentially haunted, and seemingly bad luck for everyone who entered it. Well, the simple answer is, it was cheap. I've always been sceptical about that kind of thing. Although I must admit, the first time I stood in front of the place, I did think 'what the hell have I done?' I didn't even look inside before I bought it.

If you're wondering, yes, I am now the longest-lived person that has been in this house. I've been here going on four years now, although I've fallen way behind with the repairs. *YouTube* wasn't as useful as I'd hoped.

The first time I opened the front door, a huge spider ran across my foot. I nearly quit right then and there, but I am a strong independent woman who don't need no man to squish my spiders. Sounds good right? Unfortunately, that was confined to my head, and I ran around the garden convinced it was in my shoe, screaming and jumping on one foot. Having calmed myself down, I went back inside and was immediately hit by the immense beauty of the central staircase.

Maple wood, intricate swirls carved into the wooden banisters going up the stairs. No carpet on the stairs either, just pure original wood. As I looked around the entrance hall, I walked through at least three full doorway sized cobwebs, had varying degrees of panic attack, and found my way to the kitchen.

I love the kitchen floor in this house. White marble, with beautiful matching maple wood from the stairs found in the skirting boards running around the edges. Despite the age of this house, I mean it's over 200 years old, and has spent over half its life empty, the marble floor always looks clean.

Seriously, I've lived here four years and it's the only part of the house that seems to shine at all times. My first night here, I slept in the front room, because despite my scepticism, there was a part of me that was convinced I was going to be eaten by a demon or something. I think the only reason I made it through the night was because of how tired I was from all the stressing out before I arrived, because what I found the next morning would surely have kept me up all night.

The sun streamed through the window and woke me up around eight in the morning, and the sound of the paper hitting the door jolted me upright like a jack-in-the-box. When my eyes finally focussed, I noticed the rug in the middle of the floor had been kicked over in the corner. I just assumed that I'd done it in the night and not noticed, but when I moved to the kitchen to make a coffee, I saw that all the cupboard doors were wide open.

Having been pretty sure I'd not put my collection of three plates and two mugs on display before I went to sleep, I walked towards the cupboards to close them. As I did so, a loud bang came from the front room. I jumped, hit my head on one of the cupboard doors, and tentatively moved my way back in the direction of the noise. I peered around the doorway and tried to see where the noise had come from. I couldn't see anything out of place at first, but then noticed an old dusty drinks cabinet in the far-right hand side of the room, had been flung open against the wall.

As I moved towards the cabinet, from behind me, an almighty bang caused me to leap forwards, catch my foot in the upturned corner of the rug, and go flying into the coffee table.

I've had bruised knees before, but I've never put my knee through an entire solid wooden coffee table before. That shit hurt. I swore profusely for a few minutes, and gradually hobbled my way back towards the kitchen, now on full alert.

As I moved round the corner, I saw something shift in the corner of my eye, back near the staircase. But I ignored it and moved back into the kitchen, where to my horror, all the cupboard doors had blown open again. Hesitant to go near them, I began to back away, and again, saw something move out of the corner of my eye. I snapped my head back around, and sat on the top stair of the staircase, was a doll.

A small figurine, porcelain, red hair, blue chequered dress, just sat there, arms out to the side. I wanted to go closer and investigate, and at the same time, wanted to run out of that house immediately. Things intensified, when I reached the foot of the staircase, and the kitchen cupboards started banging constantly, opening, and closing. I shot a look at the kitchen, and then shot my gaze back to the stairs, and the doll was gone.

The banging stopped, and as I looked back to the kitchen, another doll was sat on the kitchen counter. This one was in a red flowery dress, black hair, again, porcelain construction. Sat there, staring at me. I decided enough was enough, and I made for the front door, passing the first doll on my way out, which was now sat on the middle stair. I flew out the door and ran for the library.

Picking up a coffee on my way to try and calm my nerves, too early for a whiskey of course, I pawed through all the online articles about the house that I could. I read about the families and their children, the British man, the dolls, and I convinced myself that no amount of skill development or money return would make me go back there. But then I came across details of the architect who designed and built the house, and I changed my mind.

Henry Robert Stevenson had designed the house to be his home. He'd been a miner for twenty years, making a meagre income to support his wife and sick child. One day, there was a collapse in one of the mines, and he decided that if anything happened to him, his family would be left alone, and without support, his daughter wouldn't get the medicine she needed. In his spare time, he used to draw with charcoal he found in the mine, or the pieces of burnt wood from the explosions that would extend the tunnels.

He decided to put pencil to paper and design a house and build it himself. A home that wouldn't cost much and would be his haven for his family. He thought maybe if people liked the design, he could design houses for other families, and finally make a decent wage for himself. However, just before he began work on the house, his daughter passed away.

Distraught at losing her only child, his wife died just two days later, reportedly of a broken heart. Stevenson went into a downwards spiral for months afterwards, but he pulled himself together, and decided to build the house he had envisaged and to live in it in memory of his family. He worked from morning until night on the house, and all day long, he would carry around in his tool belt, his daughter's favourite dolly, to remind him why he was doing the work.

In late summer of 1806, the house was finished. However, Stevenson never got to live in the house. When leaving to get food on the day construction was completed, he was beaten to death in front of the house by a gang of pickpockets, who thought he might have valuables on him. Finding nothing, they took the dolly, and left him dead in the street. An hour later, the three killers were found dead two streets away, splayed out in the street, and sat in the centre, was the dolly of Stevenson's daughter.

Investigating the house following Stevenson's murder, the law men decided to place the doll in the house in tribute to the work Stevenson had achieved, and of course he had no family remaining. The house went up for sale to pay for his gravestone and burial, and the following year, the first family moved in.

We know how that went.

After learning this, I felt different about the house. Like there was a newfound sympathy within me. Maybe the house was haunted by Stevenson, and the dolls represented his daughter's favourite toy. Maybe the daughter was the one haunting the house, and maybe she just needed reassurance that her father loved her very much. Either way, that night, I went home to the house. As I approached the path leading to the door, I noticed the attic light was on. I froze on the spot, staring up at the window, and there staring back at me, were the two dolls from earlier, and I saw a shadow pass in the room behind them.

Fearing someone was in the house, I phoned the police, who said they would send someone round shortly. That's cop code for 'you're wasting our time.'

I moved up to the front door, opened it, and went inside, closing the door behind me. Four dolls were sat at various points on the staircase, all different shapes and sizes, different clothes, different construction, two were cloth, two were plastic. As I gradually shifted towards the kitchen, I turned and sat in the doorway was a seventh doll. A rather well-dressed male doll, complete with suit and top hat.

I changed direction again, heard a shuffle, and as I turned around yet again, the dolls on the staircase had vanished. More noise, another shooting glance, and the well-dressed doll had gone. The light in the upstairs hallway came into life, and then I noticed two of the dolls were sat with their legs dangling between the rails on the upstairs banister.

Again, I saw a shadow pass along the corridor, and against my better judgement, decided to follow it. I made my way up the stairs, one at a time, each step creaking loudly. As I moved up them, the two dolls sat on the landing turned their heads to follow me. A deep, ice-cold shiver ran down my spine and I stopped dead. Then I heard a stair creak behind me. I turned around slowly and three steps behind me, stood the well- dressed doll, top hat now in its hands, and a grin on its porcelain face.

Terrified to my very core, I turned and ran up the rest of the staircase, and down the corridor, noises and what sounded like running footsteps behind me. I reached the main bedroom door, and went to turn into it, only to see the other two dolls that had previously occupied the stairs, now sat on the bed, also with wide grins now etched onto their faces. I continued my sprint through the house and found myself running up the stairs towards the attic. The footsteps behind me grew louder, but I dared not look back for fear of what I would see.

I burst into the attic, once again in darkness, and slammed the door shut behind me, and sat behind it, ear pressed to the door.

I heard footsteps slowly moving towards the door, but there was a different tone this time. They weren't coming from the other side of the door; they were coming from within the attic.

I reached for my phone, only to realise I'd left it in the library. I gradually tried to reach for the light switch, but it was too far.

As the footsteps grew closer, I could only watch and wait for the inevitable. But nothing happened. The footsteps stopped. All I could hear was the sound of my own breathing and the thumping of my heart in my head. I tried to stop breathing so heavily and held my breaths in.

Then I realised, I could still hear heavy breathing. I turned my head to the right, and directly in front of my face was the face of Henry Robert Stevenson. I screamed, and hurled myself backwards into a pile of boxes, and hit my head on a solid wood music box. Everything became clouded and my vision blurred.

When my sight cleared up, I found myself sat on the staircase. I tried to move but I couldn't. The house was quiet, but I could see flashing lights outside. A moment later there was a knock on the door, and as it opened, I could see a police officer.

"Thank God you're here, I think there's a dead guy in the attic!" I screamed.

But the officer ignored me and continued to look around. A second officer came in and moved towards the kitchen.

"Hello? Anyone home?" Both officers called out to me.

"I'm right here, I think I hurt my head, or my back, I can't move," I said.

Still, the officers didn't respond, they were too far out of earshot. A moment later, the first officer emerged from the front room, and began climbing the stairs.

"Hey Peterson, take a look at this creepy doll here."

The officer walked up to me, picked me up in one hand, and examined me like a rag doll. The second officer came to meet him, and he passed me over to her. I couldn't move, and I couldn't speak. And in the corner of the landing, stood Henry Robert Stevenson, holding his daughters dolly, surrounded by another eight dolls, all staring back at me, smiling.

I spent the first two years in the attic, before Henry taught me how to move around. That's how long it took for the police or anyone else to notice I was missing. Clearly loved by the people. Eventually, I found that if I could picture a part of the house, and I concentrated hard, I'd find myself there. He would wander the house and spend hours looking through the windows, watching people go by, seeing if there were any more people, he could collect to expand his family.

His daughter Sarah showed me how I could manipulate things for fun. I managed to slam a few cupboards a few weeks ago. My three plates and two mugs still proudly on display. But I need to make sure I look my best for next Friday. A new family is moving in. Seems like a nice bunch. They have four kids.

Two girls, two boys.

I've always wanted a brother.

RED SNOW

'Twas the eve before Christmas, and all through
    the town,
The misery of the season was dragging folks
    down.
Financial worries and concerns about death,
Were scaring the elderly, some taking their last
    breath.

The ground thick with ice, and slippery as can be,
Steam rising from the grates, the air thick, and
    foggy.
The snow falling, blanketing everything in sight,
Preparing for the evil, which stalked through the
    night.

For you see vengeance was coming, upon
    Christmas night,
A deep, violent vengeance packed full of fright.
For the evil that's found, within everyone,

Was proving to one man, to make him come
    undone.

For Jack Marsters' mind, was preoccupied,
With the images of all the children who'd died.
His bloodthirsty actions, three years ago,
Had sunken this creature to a new all-time low.

Boiling in anger, and without thinking it
    through,
He'd targeted a businessman, a crook who he
    knew.
The crook who had promised him an abundance
    of wealth,
Had robbed him of his money, and his mental
    health.

Taken for a ride, and with nothing left,
Completely alone, and completely bereft.

His life was in tatters, his home lost as well,
He vowed to send this businessman straight
    down to hell.
He knew where this businessman set up his
    office,
But Jack was not a criminal, at this he was a
    novice.

So along came our Jack, armed with a jerry can,
Full of fuel, ready to burn, and a match in his
    hand.
He broke through the window, and set up his
    plan,
Jack was convinced he could finish this man.

Burn down his business, and take all his wealth,

And he too, would spend his days, with poor
    mental health.
With no livelihood, home, or office to work in,
This man would not even have a pot left to
    piss in.
Then he would know, just what he had done,
To Jack, who was broken, and would finally
    have won.

But as I had mentioned at the start of this plan,
Jack was a novice, and not a meticulous man.
He set up the trap, with a trail of fuel,
And went back outside to witness the duel,
Of fire against mortar, what glee he would see,
But hadn't checked on the other building in the
    vicinity.

As he lit the match, and the fire flew,
The building caught and the fire grew.
The windows blew out, and Jack watched with
    glee,
As the fire moved through the second storey.
Now completely ablaze, consumed by the flame,
Jack could hear someone calling their mother's
    name.

For Jack hadn't checked that building nearby,
And as the flames grew, the children did die,
Because behind the offices that Jack set aflame,
Was a children's hospital, St Vincent's was its
    name.

The fire spread quickly, destroying the place,
And the look of horror took over Jack's face.
The screams filled his head, his eyes locked on the
    scene,

And the office besides him started to lean.

It fell with a crash, the rubble continued to
    crackle,
And driven by madness, Jack started to cackle.
His face now contorted, what started as fun,
Had ended in murder, just what had he done?
He managed to raise himself from the ground,
And as the sirens came closer, his span himself
    round.

He ran from the scene, as fast as he could go,
For he now feared, he would be dragged down
    below.
He'd wanted revenge, but gone too far,
And distracted by terror, ran in front of a car.

Flying up over the roof, and landing hard on the
    ground,
His vision was blurred, he could hear just one
    sound,
The screams of the children, strong in his mind,
He passed into a coma, but the driver was kind.
She picked up his body, and put him in her car,
And drove him to hospital, it wasn't very far.

He woke two weeks later, confused but alive,
But right there in his head, the voices did thrive.
The children were dead, all one-hundred-three,
And were now in his mind, spreading like roots
    of a tree.

He screamed and he shouted, and begged for
    mercy,
"Why, oh why would the Gods go and curse me?
All I wanted was to put things right,

Why did I cause so much death on that night?"

The nurses, concerned for his abject behaviour,
Suggested he be committed, the doctors in
    favour.
So off Jack went, voices raging in his head,
He wished the car had killed him, so he too
    would be dead.

But the fates had other plans, as Jack would
    eventually see,
After three years of isolation, those fates set him
    free.
Times had changed, and buildings moved on,
The site of the fire, all evidence gone.

Stood on the spot of the terrorist act,
A toy shop of such grandeur, with people, was
    packed.
St Vincent's Emporium, was the name of the
    store,
Labelled with the tagline, 'no child could want
    more.'
Named after the hospital, in memory of the kids,
Such happiness inside, evil, it forbids.

But Jack did not know, until he walked by,
And the glow of the lights in the night caught
    his eye.
Gradually coming to terms with himself,
He saw models of reindeer, and Santa and an elf.

It was nearly Christmas, that most wonderful
    time,
But there is no room for joy in this terror-based
    rhyme.

Jack looked in the windows at parents delighted,
At the children inside, laughing, excited.
The voices still present, like a choir in his head,
He still saw the hospital, and all the young dead.

The image burned into the back of his mind,
Hitting his head, teeth starting to grind,
"Get out of my brain, I didn't mean to do it!"
Jack attracted some looks, but the screams
    wouldn't quit.

They'd tortured him daily, for the past three
    years,
Through anger, and laughter, and sleep, and
    through tears.

He ran down the street, as fast as he could,
To his new place of living, a house made of
    wood.
A place of sanctuary, for those just released,
Inside were the owners, preparing a feast.

Turkey, and stuffing, and all the trimmings,
And lots of people sat around the dinner table
    grinning.
Jack walked through the door, and checked
    himself in,
Turned down the food and faked a small grin.
He went to his room, and lay on the bed,
And listened to the screams, of one-hundred-
    three dead.

Jack soon drifted off, drained from exhaustion,
But at four in the morning, he heard a
    commotion.

He climbed out of bed, and walked onto the
    landing,
In front of him, six feet away, a child was
    standing.
Clutching a teddy bear, and wearing one slipper,
The child was tiny, just a sweet little nipper.
He motioned to Jack to follow his lead,
He didn't want to follow, but his mind had the
    need,
To follow this child, as if led on a leash,
Past the table with turkey, and stuffing, and
    quiche.
Out of the door, the child ten steps ahead,
Jack wondered if he was real, or one of the dead.

Completely enveloped by some kind of trance,
In the distance, another child doing a dance.
Outside of the toy store, a group were waiting,
Jack walked past a drunken man on the floor,
    defecating.
Gun shots in the distance, could not stop his
    stride,
Nor the sound of a woman, singing with pride.

The bars, they were closing, the town going to
    sleep,
Now slowing down, Jack started to creep.

The child reached the others, and they all went
    inside,
Without opening the door, and they all went to
    hide.
Jack reached the main entrance, no sign of the
    children,
Terrified, and down his back he felt a chill run.

The lights were now out, the place cloaked in
    darkness,
Jack stood on some glass and swore at its
    sharpness.
Blood trickled from his foot as he leaned on the
    door,
Which swung open at his touch, and he fell to
    the floor.
He hit his head on a wooden music box,
And rolled over to the side, to face a plush fox.

The door closed behind him, with a will of
    its own,
And the intentions of the store began to make
    their plans known.

The lock clicked fast, trapping Jack in,
And a light came on, although very dim.
Jack pulled himself to his feet, clutching his head,
And saw an outline, of a man he thought dead.

Stood near a dolls house, was the sharp
    businessman,
That started this all, so Jack turned and ran.
For the children were not the only ones lost in
    the fire,
The businessman was asleep after a late meeting
    with a supplier.

Jack banged on the door, to be let out,
He screamed, and he hollered, and continued to
    shout.
"Let me out, let me go, please God I didn't
    know!"
But nobody could hear him through the wind
    and the snow.

He felt a hand on his shoulder, and as he spun
    round,
He faced no shadow, but an object on the
    ground.
He picked up the object, a name plate of sorts,
Read 'St Vincent's Hospital', Jack's head full of
    thoughts,
Of the night of the fire, and the years that
    followed,
And the loss of life, and his mind as it hollowed.

The sound of a fire truck made him jump with
    alert,
His foot still bleeding, now starting to hurt.
The blood ran across the floor, towards the vents
    in the wall,
Where something was roaring, not pleasant at all.

Jack stumbled along, to the sound of a song,
That was coming from a teddy bear, but the
    sound was all wrong.

The words were not those of a sweet children's
    toy,
But from those of a child who'd been deprived of
    their joy.
"Why did you kill us, we burned on the fire,
You murdered us all, on that great deadly pyre,
We did nothing to you, but you killed us the
    same,
And never again will you not know our names."

The toys came to life, each one chanting a name,
Megan, and Lisa, and Alfie, and Shane,
Jason, and Mary and Alex, Chantelle,
Harry, and Owen, Noah, and Estelle.

The names, they grew louder, all the toys coming
    to life,
Moving towards him, increasing his strife.
Jack tried retreating backwards, but they were all
    around,
Toys moving everywhere, they moved to
    surround,
The mass child killer, his heart now pounding,
A ventriloquist doll's voice began sounding.

"It's time for you Jack, to face what you've done,
And accept the facts you've tried years to shun,
You burned us alive, you slaughtered us all,
And now you shall answer the Devil's call.

He waits for you Jack, in the fire down below,
And on behalf of us all, it's to hell you must go."
The heart in Jack's chest was now ready to burst,
But the toys were not done with their vengeful
    blood thirst.
Every toy in the store was now closing in,
And Jack was encompassed by the feeling of sin.

His soul felt the heat of the fire from hell,
And the midnight church bells sounded his death
    knell.
The children appeared in the store one by one,
They glowed in the light of the moon as it shone.
Jack's feet started burning, like standing on sand,
In the heat of the desert in a faraway land.

The kids started chanting, as Jack's nose started
    bleeding,
Their long-waited vengeance was finally
    succeeding.

Jack screamed in pain, as heat blistered his skin,
And he felt his lungs turning to liquid within.
The children continued to sing their deadly
    rhyme,
of Ring-Around-The-Roses, taking their time,
To enjoy their revenge from beyond the grave,
For now, nothing earthly, Jack's life, could it save.

His face began melting, as the flames started
    rising,
The speed of the fire was very surprising.
The toys began melting as the children
    watched on,
They would watch the man burn, until he was
    gone.
Jack's screams rang out all through the night,
The sound of agony, and pain, and of fright.
The store became engulfed, in a matter of
    minutes,
But didn't expand beyond the store's footprint
    limits.
And through all the fire, the dancing of flames,
The children stood watching, chanting their
    names.

As Jack finally descended into the pits of hell,
The flames, and the heat began slowly to quell.
Watching from behind the children, stood the
    sharp businessman,
Everything finally, had gone according to plan.

For Jack was a novice, in life and in death,
And that crucial mistake, cost him his last breath.

As the fire went out, and the rubble crackled,

The children, and the businessman, together,
    they cackled.
The businessman, led them, he turned to go,
Leaving nothing behind but a red tint in the
    snow.
The children turned too, their revenge they had
    taken,
And walked away, leaving one person shaken.
As they vanished into the cold of the night,
I stood there, still, frozen with fright.

My name is Duncan, the owner of the store,
And this tale will stay with me, forevermore.
The night that I saw the gates open to hell,
And the fire, and vengeance and that burning
    smell.
The tale of a man who'd been racked with such
    guilt,
Drawn in by the spirits of those whose blood he
    had spilt.

And now as I work to rebuild my store,
I know the children are at peace, Forevermore.

GALAXY OF PAIN

Silence. The only sounds that were audible was the gentle beeping of machinery and consoles in the background. A low, blue glow emitted from the lights illuminating the corridor.

Everything was on minimal power. No power had been given to unessential systems. It was vital that nothing interfered with the journey, and its primary goal.

It was a system that had been used countless times, for billions of people across hundreds of years. And yet, this time felt different. The consoles and systems were now ancient. There were drips from the ceiling panels, where water filtration systems had failed. The doors in the sleeping quarters were permanently jammed open, not that they were needed.

The Raven had been in service for seven hundred and forty- nine years, and eleven months. That's a long time for a passenger transport ship. But in just four weeks' time, she would arrive at her destination for the final time. No empty journeys back to Earth, one hundred and fifty years on auto pilot in each direction. She would finally be at ease. There was nothing to go back for.

Everyone was now gone, Earth was a desolate wasteland, and there was no going back.

The Raven meandered her way through the emptiness day after day, automatic diagnostics going on in the background, a quiet voice murmuring course corrections, as the ship adjusted headings to avoid asteroids and comets. The computer had nobody to talk to but itself.

You would never guess that the ship was carrying eighty-six people. They were the best of the best, the ones who stayed behind, and risked their lives to ensure everyone made it off the Earth, and onto the ship towards salvation on Titan.

Named after Saturn's moon, the planet was perfect. Picked up by a scouting vessel nearly a millennia before, the decision was made to begin sending scientists out there to explore. Nobody conceived of the horrors that would force them to send the entire population. The people of Earth spent so many hundreds of years worrying about climate change, and trying to fix the damage they had done, that they were completely unprepared for an attack from above.

In the years following what was dubbed 'The Decimation', the remaining leaders banded together to find another home before the core of the planet destabilised and humanity would be lost forever. Titan was that place. The only downside being, that it took one hundred and fifty years to reach at available speeds. A fleet of seven ships were built, complete with cryogenic stasis pods to keep the crews in suspended animation for most of the journey. They would remain awake for the first year of the trip, to ensure all systems were completely functional, and the last two weeks to prepare the ship for arrival and ensure everything was on course during the final approach.

Six of the seven ships were built to house over ten thousand passengers and were named after some of history's greatest figures. *Einstein, Hawking, Galileo, Curie, Shakespeare,* and the *Rosa Parks*. The seventh ship, the Raven, was built to accommodate only two hundred passengers, and would be used as a crew transport, shipping staff back and forth during the transition. However, after the first two trips, the situation on Earth became more intensely acute and the planet began decaying at a faster rate, so another one-hundred-and-twenty ships were put onto the express line and built quickly over the next ten years, all named after vessels from favourite TV shows or movies.

Ships led by the *Phoenix*, the *Milano*, and of course, the *Enterprise* left Earth in a huge convoy, the largest departure mankind had ever undertaken. One-hundred-twenty ships each with a capacity of thirty-thousand passengers. Even that was tight going, because whilst over three quarters of the planet's population had been decimated, the journey time meant that often, ships would have to travel over capacity, and a rotating stasis schedule would be put in place. In the end, over seventy thousand people died making the trips on the vessels with too many occupants.

History dictates that maiden or final journeys seldom pass without incident, and this final journey would be no different. Without warning, the silence on board the *Raven* was shattered by an almighty explosion from the starboard side. The ship veered off course, and the alert sirens sounded.

"Alert level 1, emergency revival procedures initiated. Shields in operation, weapons on standby."

Another jolt hit the ship, this time from the port side.

"Hull has been breached. Emergency forcefields are now active. Power reserves down to seventy-nine percent. Estimated time to failure, four minutes, twenty seconds."

The fire suppression systems activated, filling the corridor with white smoke. From within the smoke, came the sound of coughing and spluttering. A hand emerged, and slapped the bulkhead, the arm trying to secure balance against the rocking of the vessel.

Commander Mace Jackson fell to the ground as the next hit blew another hole in the side of the *Raven*.

"Warning, second hull breach, deck seven. Emergency forcefields will fail in two minutes, fifteen seconds. Command assistance required."

Mace hauled himself up from the deck plates, vision still blurry, not completely sure of his surroundings. He tried to make sense of the chaos surrounding him. He moved down the corridor towards the stairs. In the back of his mind, he knew the elevators would not be functional during an attack, and his instinct was to get to the bridge. He found his voice and uttered his first words for nearly a century and a half.

"Raven, situation report."

"Good day Commander. We are currently under attack from a Decimator ship, approximately seventeen life signs on board. Our shields are down to fifty-four percent, and life support has failed on decks four through

seven. Weapons systems are still operational, however I am unable to initiate counter offence manoeuvres, as my systems have been damaged."

"Jesus Christ, decks four through seven? *Raven*, what about the crew?" Mace continued up the final flight of stairs nearing the bridge but feared for his officers and crew below.

"I am unable to scan those decks to determine the level of casualties, as we sustained a hull breach in sections four, seven and eight of those decks."

"But those are the areas with the cryo-pods?"

"That is correct Commander. Whilst I am unable to determine the degree of loss, the chances of the crew surviving that level of damage are negligible."

Mace burst onto the bridge just in time to see the Decimator ship making another run. He threw himself down into the pilot seat, and strapped in.

"Raven, transfer weapons controls to the helm, and prepare to engage manual override."

"Manual override is available, and weapons controls are now at your disposal."

"Let's see if I remember how to fight."

Mace ran his fingers over the console, flinging the *Raven* into a spiral, dodging the enemy weapons fire as they flew above.

Bringing the ship back around to face the Decimators, Mace brought the targeting systems online.

"Raven, I want multiple target locks. Save each input in sequence, and when I give the order, fire all weapons at those targets."

"Inputs have been recorded. Ready to execute on your command."

The ship closed in and was nearing point blank range.

"FIRE!" Mace bellowed the command, and tapped on the console's controls frantically, piloting the *Raven* upside down, and as it passed over the top of the enemy vessel, *Raven* fired all its weapons hitting each critical system with everything she had. As Mace brought the *Raven* back around, the Decimator ship exploded in a huge firework display of green and yellow light, and Raven sailed through the debris and continued on course.

Breathing a sigh of relief, Mace now began to understand the realisation that he may now be alone on board the *Raven*.

"Raven, are you able to ascertain the casualties yet?"

"Attempting to bypass damaged systems. Please stand by Commander."

Mace thought of everything he had been through with the crew. Three trips in suspended animation, no issues. Watching the atmosphere of the planet he'd called home burn into nothingness as they broke orbit for the final time. He glanced down at the chronometer. Three weeks. They only had three weeks left, and they'd have made it.

"Systems bypassed Commander. Internal sensors show that of the eighty-five currently occupied cryo-pods, sixty-two have been lost to the hull breach and are no longer aboard the ship. Of the twenty-four remaining on board, there are two left in partial operation, those of Lieutenant Jennifer Holden, and Engineer Robert Green. They are the only two remaining life signs on board besides your own."

Mace pondered this for a moment. His entire crew were gone. They'd travelled one-hundred-forty-nine years and been taken just three weeks from the end. Murdered in their sleep.

Decimated.

"Raven, are the hull breaches contained?"

All Mace's emotions were flooding to the surface, but they were still in trouble. He had to get the situation under control. There would be time to mourn when they reached Titan.

"The hull breaches are contained for now Commander, but they will not hold without diverting power from the life support from the lower decks. And the two cryo-pods are failing. I suggest the occupants are removed immediately. They have only ninety-seconds of life support remaining."

Mace dragged himself to his feet and began leaping down the stairs back towards the room he had been released from just minutes earlier. The ship still rocked from the resulting damage of the attack. He rounded the corridor towards the stasis room on deck three and stopped in his tracks.

Standing at the entrance, was his former Captain, Edward Martin. Edward had been the first casualty of the mission, after a conduit ruptured on the bridge just three weeks into the journey. And yet here he was, staring back at Mace, his skin white as a sheet, uniform stained with blood. Mace was frozen to the spot.

"Cryo-pods will lose life support in sixty seconds."

The words only just resonated with Mace, still staggered at the sight before him. A chill ran down his spine as Martin spoke to him.

"You must turn back, Mace. You must turn away from Titan."

The figure of his former Captain turned away from him and walked slowly into the stasis room.

"Cryo-pods will lose life support in thirty seconds."

Mace sprinted into the room, but Martin was gone. He looked frantically across the whole area but there was no sign of the captain. He pushed what he had seen to the back of his mind and made his way towards the pod where Jennifer was. But here he faced a dilemma. Jennifer's pod was on the other side of the room to Roberts. He could only try to save one.

"Cryo-pods will lose life support in ten seconds. Nine. Eight. Seven..."

Making the choice that Jennifer was closer, Mace leapt over the pod next to her and punched in the controls to open the door.

But the mechanism was jammed.

"Five. Four. Three."

Mace punched in the revival code, and Jennifer's eyelids started to open, but her couldn't get the door open. She looked at him and raised her hand to the glass.

"Mace?"

"Two. One. Life support has failed."

Mace watched as Jennifer began suffocating. Her hands clasped her throat before flying up at the glass. Mace punched the controls, but they still wouldn't give.

On the other side of the room, he could here Robert suffocating too. Mace began punching the glass with his fists, but he couldn't even make a crack. As Jennifer's body became limp, and the last gasp of air escaped her mouth, she looked directly at him, her eyes penetrating his own. Her hand slid down the glass to fall at her side, and the computer registered her life signs had gone. On the other side of the room, the same sound emanated from Robert's pod. Mace had tried to save one of them and ended up saving neither. He was alone now.

"You need to turn away Mace. Turn the ship around."

The voice made him snap his head around. But there was nobody there. Again, a whisper came from behind him.

"Turn the *Raven* away. Fly her home."

Again, he snapped around, and again, there was nobody there.

"Who's there!" he shouted. Sweat began trickling down his forehead, and a cold sweat formed down his back. "Show yourself!"

He felt a cold hand on his shoulder, span around, nothing. Again, a tight grip on his other shoulder, span around, nobody there.

"*Raven*, are there any life signs on board besides me?"

"Negative Commander. You are the only remaining lifeform on board."

"What is the location of Captain Edward Martin's body?"

"Captain Martin's remains are in the Cargo Bay, where they have been held since you placed them there."

Mace had to see for himself. He turned back to look at Jennifer, her eyes still wide open. A single tear fell down his left cheek, but he blinked it away and left the room to see if the captain was indeed where he had left him. As he walked away from the stasis room, he was watched by a pair of unseen eyes. As he rounded the corner, Jennifer walked out of the room to follow him.

Mace stood over the cryo-pod staring down at his Captain. His eyes were closed, his skin pale, his arms crossed over his chest, in full uniform, just as Mace had laid him out over a century ago.

"How the hell did I see you standing in front of me Ed? You spoke to me. Am I losing my mind? I am the only one left after all. I don't know what to do. They're all gone Ed, everyone.

What should I do?" "*Turn back.*"

The whisper came from the doorway, and Mace bolted upright, one hand still on the side of the pod, one hand reaching for a nearby metal pipe.

"Who's there?" Mace asked into the darkness, only penetrated by the glow of the two red doorway lights.

No response.

"I must be losing it."

He ran his hand through his hair and over his head checking for any sign of head trauma but found none. Then the glass under his hand vibrated sharply. He jumped, and as he looked down, Edward Martin was staring back at him, eyes wide open. Mace flew backwards, cascading into the shelving and sending the whole thing crashing down onto the floor. He gradually got to his feet, and moved back towards the pod, and glanced over.

Captain Martin was back in position, eyes closed, hands across his chest.

"Fly the raven home, mace. Turn back now. You must turn back."

"WHO ARE YOU!"

Mace yelled and picked up a piece of the broken shelving, and began smashing containers, kicking over shelving units.

"WHERE ARE YOU, YOU SON OF A BITCH!"

Mace continued his rampage, moving towards the doorway. He smashed the piece of shelving into the comms panel sending sparks flying everywhere and stopped dead in his tracks. Stood in the doorway less than two feet away, were Jennifer and Robert. Hands drooped at their sides, skin pale, eyes wide.

"Turn the ship around Mace. You're too late. We all died, don't let yourself die too."

Jennifer's voice was cold and forced, like she had been choked. "Yes Mace, it's too late. Fly the *Raven* home."

Rogers' voice was also horse, and raspy. Mace was frozen in place yet again, but he managed to speak, and didn't let his gaze wander for a nanosecond.

"How are you here? I saw you die?"

Another tear made its way down his cheek, followed by another.

"Just fly her home, Mace."

Jennifer and Robert moved into the corridor, and Mace flew after them, but they were gone.

Mace had been staring out of the window on the bridge for eight hours, contemplating what he'd seen, what had happened. The computer consoles beeped in acknowledgement as he entered the course corrections to keep them on course to Titan.

His reflection stared back at him amongst the stars, his mind wandering to the Christmas party the week before they all entered stasis. Jennifer had given him the eye while he was toasting the crew. He'd made it his mission that when they woke up, he'd take her out to dinner. He thought back to his promotion ceremony on Earth, when Captain Martin was given command of the *Raven*, and enlisted Mace as his second in command.

He was so proud having worked so hard helping to design the colony ships and ensuring as many people got on board as possible for each trip. There was never any empty seats or pods on his watch. He worked with these people across nearly five centuries through space and time, and now they were all gone.

His head sunk, to look at the console. Three-fifty-seven in the morning. But he had no appetite for sleep. He'd been asleep for nearly a century and a half, and after the experiences he'd had in the last twenty-four hours, there was no chance of catching forty winks. Still, he thought, he should get on with repairing *Raven's* autopilot, so he could start the other major repairs.

There were still three weeks before the ship reached Titan. And yet he couldn't help pondering the words that kept being repeated to him over and over.

Turn back. It's too late. Fly the Raven home.

What did they mean? Too late for what? The only answer he had was to reach Titan and find out, but as he looked back up at the window, his wasn't the only reflection staring back at him.

His navigation officer, Grant Sanderson was mouthing words, but Mace couldn't make them out. He turned around, but Grant wasn't there. He stood up and walked towards where his reflection had showed him standing. Seeing nothing, he turned around and came face to face with Grant. His eyes were void, skin as pale as the others. He grabbed Mace's shirt and pulled his decaying face close to his and repeated the words.

"TURN BACK! TURN BACK! IT'S TOO LATE!"

He shook Mace violently as he shouted the words, pain spreading across his face, like he was being tortured. Mace broke free of his icy grip and fell backwards to the floor hitting his head on the metal deck plate. Through his blurred vision, he saw that Grant had gone, but as he passed out of consciousness, he saw Jennifer standing in the corner of the room. As his eyes closed, she mouthed the words 'turn back', and then everything went black.

A splitting pain went through Mace's head as he roused himself from the floor. He patted his hand to the back of his neck, and felt dried blood, his hair also matted with it. He pulled himself across the floor to the pilot chair and hauled himself up into it. As his vision began returning, he glanced at the chronometer.

He'd been out for nearly twelve hours. He gave a look of disbelief and felt his head again.

"Well, that would explain why it's dry," he mused, as he tugged clumps of the dried blood from his hair. He remembered the chilling words that had been shaken into him by his dead crewmate and repeated again by Jennifer.

'*Turn back. Fly the Raven home.*'

Something was trying to warn him about the trip ahead. What had happened? Were they the spirits of his dead crew or was he going insane. He'd had at least two blows to the head, so it was possible he was injured more than he thought. The only way he was going to get answers would be to reach his destination and see for himself.

Suddenly, the comms panel burst into life.

"*Commander, we are receiving and automated message. It is from Titan.*"

Mace looked at the panel and confirmed that it did indeed originate on Titan.

"*Raven*, play the message on the screen."

A woman's face appeared on the monitor. She was about thirty- five years of age, long brown hair, in full uniform, bearing the insignia of an Admiral. Behind her was a huge glass window overlooking a park, with the logo of the Colonisation Fleet at the centre of a giant fountain. She began to speak.

"Raven, this is Admiral Nadia Rochenko calling you from the new headquarters of the Colonisation Fleet on Titan. On behalf of us all, I would like to welcome you into the system, and inform you that we here cannot wait for you to come home.

As you can see behind me, Titan is thriving, and we are all so excited for the final mission of the Raven to be concluded.

Upon arrival, you will be met by our highest-ranking officials, and escorted to your debriefing, where you will be assigned your homes, and your work assignments. Titan has been flourishing for nearly three centuries now. We have entire families created on this world, and it has become a Haven for not only us, but other species within the system seeking refuge.

There are now six different species living on Titan in perfect harmony. Whilst we know leaving Earth was difficult, it was our only choice, and has proven to be the right one. We eagerly await your arrival. Message ends."

Mace closed the recording and saved the file into the ship database.

"Raven are we able to reply to Titan yet?" asked Mace, fearing he already knew the answer.

"At this time Commander, the communications array is down. We are able to receive messages but not send or reply to them. However, our estimated arrival time at Titan is now only eleven days."

"11 days? When I got knocked to the floor, there was nearly three weeks. What happened?"

"We passed near to an ageing star in a state of flux and were enveloped by solar winds. They carried the ship faster than our engines are capable of for almost ten hours. As a result, our journey time has been shortened."

"Hell, I'll take any good news I can get right now."

Mace opened the supply closet next to the console and pulled out his engineer kit.

"Guess I'd better fix that comms relay then."

As he went to stand, a loud thump came from down the stairs. Mace stopped and listened quietly. Another thump. And another. Then two thumps. Mace got out of his chair and began walking towards the stairs. Another three thumps. It almost sounded like someone banking on a wall or a window. He began descending the staircase. Another two thumps. At the foot of the stairs, he entered the corridor, at the end of which was the stasis room. Another three thumps, faster this time.

He edged down the hall, feeling his way along the wall in the glow of the red emergency lights. Another four thumps, quick in succession. The noises got louder as he edged nearer to the pods. The lights in the room ahead were now completely dead. There'd been no sense in wasting energy to light a room full of dead people, so the computer had rerouted it, and initiated emergency lights only beyond the bridge. Three more thumps, much more intense this time. As Mace reached the doorway, the thumps stopped.

"*Raven*, activate the lights in Stasis Room 1."

"*I am unable to complete that request Commander, the power has been rerouted to provide additional support to the emergency forcefields surrounding the hull breaches. If I send the power back in our current condition, we could lose containment.*"

"Great, so I get to fumble in the dark."

Mace reached into his kit, and pulled out a flashlight, switching it on as he placed his kit on the ground next to the entrance. He shone his light around the room but could see nothing. The light glinted off the glass tops of the pods, each area plunging back into darkness as the light left it. He moved into the room and edged towards the centre.

A loud thump came from behind him.

He spun around and aimed his light in the direction of the noise. There was nothing. He carried on moving around the room. Another thump stopped him in his tracks. This one was nearer. Again, he shone his light, but found no source to the noise. Another thump, this time from behind him. He targeted his torch towards the noise, and again found nothing, but in the glint of the light, he could make out what looked like two handprints on the lid of one of the pods. He moved in for a closer look but was disturbed by three thumps behind him.

He spun around, and several pods were now suddenly standing upright, the lifeless bodies within all with eyes open, staring at him. More thumps, and he turned around again, to find more pods standing upright, all the bodies wide eyed and looking right at him. Suddenly, the doors closed, and Mace was plunged into darkness, with only the short-range light from his torch providing an image.

His spine chilled, and he began to fumble his way back towards the now closed door, bombarded with noises and thumps, and every time he moved his beam of light, more pods were upright, the victims staring back at him. His back hit the doors, and he began frantically punching in the codes to open them, but the negative chime of 'access denied' kept ringing out.

"Turn back. Turn the ship back. Fly the Raven home."

The voices began to chant, first one, then three, then ten, until finally, all the body's lips began to move in unison.

"Turn back Mace. It's too late. Turn away. Fly the raven home."

They all raised their fists and began thumping on the glass as they chanted louder.

"We died; don't you die too. Something is waiting for you if you do. Turn back and fly the Raven home!"

With his sixth attempt, the doors flew open, and Mace fell backwards through the door, the chants and thumps getting louder. He leapt back to his feet, and punched in the access codes again, and the doors closed, and shut out the chants and the banging.

Mace slid down against the doors and started taking deep breaths. He closed his eyes and put a hand on his chest in a conscious effort to slow his heart rate.

BANG!

A massive thud on the other side of the door shot Mace forwards in panic.

BANG!

Another thud, joined by another, and another. It sounded like the dead were trying to smash their way out of the stasis room. Mace scrambled to his feet, grabbed his kit and ran back all the way to the bridge and locked himself inside, the banging continuing in the distance.

Mace had isolated himself in the bridge for six days before the comms panel finally breathed into life. Doing the repairs remotely had taken ten times longer than if he'd have accessed the relay directly, but the horror that was plaguing him was too brutal. In those six days, he'd seen images, or spirits of ten different crew members, all telling him to turn back. He'd tried to block them out, and continue his work, but it had not been easy. Now though, he would get some answers.

"*Raven*, access the comms system, and create a link with Titan."

"*Establishing a link now Commander.*"

Nothing.

"*Commander, I am unable to establish a link with Titan.*"

"What's the reason?"

"*I am unable to determine the exact cause, but the issue appears to be with the equipment on Titan. The comms relay onboard this ship is now fully functional.*"

"Repeat attempts every fifteen minutes and notify me of any change."

Mace climbed into his makeshift hammock that he'd created from the captain's chair cushioning and the fabric of the chair from the engineering station. He closed his eyes and attempted to get some sleep, but those words kept reverberating around his mind.

Turn back. It's too late. Fly the Raven home.

Something wasn't right, that much was clear. There was no response from Titan. Surely, there was at least one transmitter working on the planet, the entire remaining population of Earth had been transported there. There was almost a billion people on Titan. Someone must be able to talk to him.

"You know we are right Mace. It's too late. Turn back." Mace didn't open his eyes.

"Jennifer, go away. You need to rest in peace. Leave me alone."

"You must turn back Mace, we all died, don't let it happen to you too."

"Jennifer, wake me up when you have some new sentences to say to me. Until then, fuck off."

Mace felt like he'd slept for days. He woke to the sound of a proximity alert. He climbed down from the hammock, Jennifer still sat in the corner, watching.

"Commander, there is a ship approaching. It appears to be of Colony Fleet design."

"Can you identify it?" Mace asked eagerly.

"It appears to be the CFS Einstein. I'm not reading any life signs on board, and they are not sending out any communications."

"Hail them, *Raven*."

"No response Commander."

Mace moved to sit in the navigation chair. He could feel Jennifer's eyes on him.

"Care to volunteer any useful information? Or are you just going to sit there like a sulking ghost?"

Mace turned to face her. She sat perfectly still but didn't offer an answer. The console panel frittered in and out of phase for a moment, before going dead completely. Mace tried to reboot it, but to no avail.

"Turn back Mace."

The computer addressed Mace directly, but it wasn't the computer he was used to.

"It's too late. Turn back and fly the raven home. Turn back."

"*Raven*, is that you?"

"Turn back, Mace!"

The panels fluttered back to life, and Mace glanced at the chronometer. It was now just four days until he reached Titan. But when he looked up, the *Einstein* was gone.

As futile as it had been, Mace spent the next four days attempting to fix the long-range sensors from inside the bridge. He still refused to go back out there amongst the dead, and even Jennifer had gotten fed up and left after two days. As strange as it may have been, Mace got used to her being there.

She had said nothing for those two days, simply sat in the corner, watching him, but it made him feel like he wasn't alone. He had failed to get the sensors working but was interrupted by the computer.

"Commander, we are approaching Titan."

Mace stood up, popped the panel back into place, and moved to the front of the bridge. Sure enough, out of the darkness of space, emerged a blue and green ball of wonder. He'd forgotten just how much like Earth Titan appeared to be from space. The continents were obviously different shapes, and there were three moons instead of one, but the similarities were uncanny. In the distance, the sun for this system shone bright and red.

"*Raven,* give me a lifesigns reading for the planet." *"I am picking up one lifesign on the surface."* Mace snapped to attention.

"What? One? Are you sure?"

"Affirmative Commander. The lifesign I am reading is the only one on the planet."

Mace slumped down into his chair. His brain was trying to process this new information. Information that as hard as it was to hear, he had suspected was true, and went back to those repeated words from the dead of the crew. *Turn back, it's too late, fly the Raven home.*

"*Raven,* are there any signs of attack, or struggle?"

Mace was desperately searching for an answer, but he didn't get one.

"Negative Commander. The planet is as described in the message from the Admiral. Negligible readings of air pollution, thriving ecosystem and stable breathable atmosphere."

"Is the lifesign human?"

"Inconclusive."

"Is it safe to go down there in a worker pod?"

"Affirmative."

"Don't go down there, Mace. Please." Mace turned to look at Jennifer.

"Please? That's a new one. Are you going to tell me what's going on? Are you really Jennifer? Are they really my crew? What happened here?"

Jennifer moved to sit in the hammock, but she just seemed to float in the air.

"I am me. At least I was. Now I'm somewhere else. We're somewhere else. We are connected to this place, but we are in another. Death happened here. You must turn back, before he sees you."

"Before whom sees me? The lifeform on the planet? Who is he?"

Jennifer curled up into a ball.

Captain Martin spoke from the doorway to the bridge.

"Mace, he will hurt you. He knows only pain. He has known pain his entire being. It is the purpose of his being, and yet he denies it, so inflicts it on all others. You must fly the *Raven* home."

"With all due respect Captain, there is no home to fly the *Raven* back to. This was supposed to be our home. The human race's new home. Where am I going to go?"

Mace was infuriated that he had to keep reminding the spirits that the only thing left in the Terran system was the Sun. There was no home to go back to. They knew that. At least, they had.

Robert was now sat in his old chair, despite the absence of the fabric.

"Sir, he is powerful. He has existed for thousands of years. He takes us, but we can speak here because of you. We have a connection to this place. It is our home."

"If the *Raven* is your home, how can I fly the *Raven* home?"

Mace was trying to piece it all together, completely oblivious to the warning light on the console behind him.

Jennifer spoke up and sat in the seat beside Mace.

"You must fly the Raven home, Mace. It is the only way you will avoid the same fate we have suffered. We exist only in pain. You must escape. If there is no Raven, there is no pain for you."

And finally, everything fell into place.

"You want me to destroy the *Raven*. Whatever this being is, what he's done to you all, it is a fate worse than death. Did he kill everyone below?"

All three spirits nodded. Martin spoke up.

"He took their existence. They now exist in a different place, only in pain. He made a mistake a long time ago, and he has been trying to fix it for centuries. It has consumed him, and everyone around him. You must fly the *Raven* home and save yourself from an existence of nothing but pain."

The warning sounds finally alerted Mace to an incoming object. He looked out of the window and saw a purple mass rising from the planet below at alarming speed, heading right towards the ship.

"It's too late. He is coming! You must fly the *Raven* home, before he takes you too! He took the Decimators, he took the humans, he took us all! You must turn away!"

Jennifer was in full panic mode. Mace turned to see the mist about to hit the ship. He locked in a new flight path, directly for the sun, and shut off the panel. The mist hit the ship like a torpedo, knocking Mace to the ground. When he got up, he was faced with a man, roughly six-four, greying hair on the sides of his head, wearing an unrecognisable red and black uniform of some sort. The three spirits of his comrades screamed out in pain and vanished.

"Oh, I think that's a little harsh. Give someone an eternity of pain, and they do nothing but cry about it."

The man leaned on the door frame and crossed his arms. Mace felt the ship turn gradually and increase speed. He decided to buy some time and learn what he could from this evil creature.

"So, you're the piece of shit that killed my crew."

"Ooh, so direct and volatile. Technically, I didn't kill them. I merely instigated the assault that delivered them into my hands. You see, my range is limited. I'm a pain wraith, not *Superman*. I wish I could fly, but alas, it is beyond me. Well not more than this short distance anyway."

"You're a what?" The man sighed.

"Look, I've told my story to people across the centuries, and to be quite frank I'm sick of it. You're the last one, and then my work will finally be done."

"What work? Captain Martin said you'd made some sort of mistake you were trying to put right?"

The man sighed and rolled his eyes, almost as if he were bored.

"I made an error of judgment over a thousand years ago, and I suffered for it. One little mistake that changed the course of time far more than I realised. I've spent the entirety of my existence since trying to wipe out all the people who shouldn't have been alive, or all the people who should never have been born, all because of one tiny pathetic little mistake, until I could come to only one conclusion. If I wiped you all out, then there would be no problems left. No humans, no consequences."

The ship began to vibrate as it approached the sun, and Mace secretly silenced the warning from the computer.

"You've destroyed us all? The whole human race?" Mace tried to make his pained voice sound even more distressed.

"Well, you're not exactly dead. Your bodies are dead, but your energy, what you pathetic little things call a soul, they still exist in my realm, where I'm from. It's an awful place, it's worse than death. Can you imagine, knowing nothing but pain forevermore? I've lived that life, and I have no intentions of ever going back. And the only way to guarantee that is to end this quest once and for all. Then I can rest."

The ship jerked violently, and a panel burst off the wall. Steam began rising from the other panels, and the computer issued a warning on the monitors. Impact was imminent. Mace stood tall, as the shaking began more violent, and the glass behind him began to crack. He faced the figure with determination and a tear in his eye.

"I don't care what you are, or what you've done. But I will tell you one thing, and one thing only."

The man looked confused, for a moment he had no response. He then noticed the ever-increasing ball of light outside the window, and a look of panic began to set in. Mace continued.

"You're not getting me."

The man leapt towards Mace, but it was too late. The ship entered the sun's corona and exploded in a magnificent ball of light. A huge violet coloured swirl emerged from the sun and headed out into space. As it moved past Titan, the planet itself faded away, and the screams of the pain wraith echoed across space and time, and there was a huge flash of light that encompassed the sky like the dawn of creation.

It had been a tough week for Alex.

He'd failed to get the new job he was being interviewed for, his existing boss had fired him for not securing a new seating deal with the local sports stadium, and he now found himself driving back home, once again at night. He'd become used to driving in the early hours, although it seemed this would be the last time. The day after he'd been fired, he'd discovered the company had gone into liquidation. Even if his boss hadn't let him go, he'd have lost his job anyway. At least Alex had a home to go to. His boss had lost his wife and kids, they'd moved out and he was all alone, and at risk of bankruptcy.

Couldn't happen to a nicer person, was the first thing Alex thought.

He was lost in his thoughts, when he realised, he was driving on the wrong side of the road, and a truck was coming towards him. The truck blared his horn, and Alex swerved out of the way. He pulled over in a layby and stopped the engine.

"I am way too tired to be driving. I'm gonna roll this thing down a cliff or something in a minute."

He pulled out his phone and loaded up Google Maps. He found a motel nearby and set directions. An hour later, he pulled into the motel car park, and checked in. The rest of his week passed without incident, and he returned home, and looked for a new job. He saw his boss had taken his own life following his family leaving him. He'd jumped off the Golden Gate bridge.

'What a way to go', he thought. 'Still, it could've been worse. He could've been pushed.'

THE GIRL IN THE MIST

"Planning is crucial, Marjorie, let us not forget that. If I hadn't planned this trip extensively, then this would be a disaster zone right now."

Jonathan Miles had been plotting every single detail of this expedition for over five years. The logistics of the transportation, the ratio of supplies needed, the potential location for the nerve centre, and of course, the backup options should anything go wrong. So, he was immensely confident and comfortable when the message arrived to say that his first choice of transport was no longer available.

"Yes, but Jonny, you're being rather selfish about the people who just died."

Marjorie wasn't particularly impressed with the outlook that Jonathan was choosing to take. After all, the reason the transport was no longer available was because the team tasked with flying them to Antarctica had been lost in a plane crash. Surely this was a time for regret and reflection. At least for most people.

"Marjorie, I can only concern myself with my own circumstances, and not those of others. This trip is too important to dwell on the trivial matters that affect other people."

Watching from the corner of the room, was Jonathan's wife Abigail. She was as unimpressed with his attitude to the deaths of seven people, as Marjorie was. But she knew that Jonathan wouldn't care much for her opinion.

He hadn't shown any interest in her at all since he'd started his affair with Marjorie. Hired to help around the mansion in the summer, it soon became obvious that there was something between the two. Marjorie was ten years younger than Abigail, at just twenty-four, and her choice of clothing and the way she presented herself made it very clear of her intentions. The nickname she used to address her employer, 'Jonny', was the biggest indication yet. The fact that Abigail had caught them kissing in the grounds, had just confirmed her suspicions.

"Oh Jonny, you can be so wicked," Marjorie said as a thin smile spread across her face.

Jonathan looked up at her, and returned the smile, before checking his watch and pausing. Neither of them noticed Abigail was even in the room as they left. Either they didn't care, or they genuinely were so wrapped up in other thoughts, that they genuinely didn't notice her. With such little interest shown to her in the last six months, Abigail had begun to spiral into a very dark place. With no family, and no friends outside of the house, she would have nowhere to go if she had chosen to leave.

She eased herself down into the wingback chair next to the bookcase, and rested her head on her hands, her eyes red from spending the morning crying, and contemplating her dilemma. How could she tell a man who clearly had no interest in her anymore, that she was pregnant with his child?

The doorbell rang, snapping Abigail out of her trance, and as she waited for the butler, Giles, to answer the door, she stood up from her chair, and waited to see who was there. Visitors were a rare occurrence to the mansion, so she took small solace in the sight of a new face. As the large oak doors swung open, a trio of men entered the house, each carrying a large bag on their backs. Abigail knew they were not here to see her, and clearly had something to do with the expedition.

Giles directed to where they could leave their equipment, and after depositing it, they turned and left. The doors were closed, and Giles returned to his duties, turning to look and smile at Abigail, as he passed by. He was the only one to give any kind of attention to Abigail, but even that seemed disconnected.

Keeping the line between employer and employee was important to people like Giles. The old guard.

Abigail was permanently shrouded in a cloak of despair, darkness, and distrust, and there was no way out for her. She felt trapped, in a house which despite not having bars on the windows, very much felt like a prison. She headed down the long hallway towards the kitchen, passing the large ornate windows overlooking the grounds as she went. Giles was now outside running the hose over the flower beds. The weather was very pleasant, clear skies, no clouds, and the temperature was in the mid-twenties. Not bad for winter. Perhaps this was why Jonathan was so desperate to find snow in the Antarctic. Maybe he would feel more at home in the cold frozen wasteland, than at home with his wife. Abigail could hear a small commotion ahead of her in the kitchen and pressed her ear to the semi-closed door. She recognised the sounds immediately, and as she opened the door, her fears were finally confirmed.

Marjorie was bent over on the kitchen counter, her hands spread across the marble, face turned to the left. Her naked breasts were being pressed into the work surface, and Jonathan was standing directly behind her, shirt open, thrusting violently. Abigail had known, of course, for months, but despite the kissing incident, she had never seen them having sex.

This was the final part of the betrayal. She watched, completely unnoticed, as Marjorie turned around, and leapt into Jonathan's arms, the two of them positioning themselves to continue.

Jonathan sat her back down on top of the counter and buried his face in Marjorie's breasts as they bounced from the act of the sex. Abigail watched on, almost as if she were a ghost and endured the whole thing. Neither of them had attempted to hide what they were doing, nor do so quietly. They simply did not care.

As Abigail finally turned away and began climbing the stairs, slowly, one by one, tears began trickling down her cheeks, but her face itself was frozen; completely numb. There was no indication of hurt or anger, only tears.

In the background, Marjorie's moans had now become audible from most rooms in the house. 'Clearly, they had not finished' thought Abigail as she continued upstairs. The true unabashed treachery of what they were doing simply didn't register to them. As Abigail reached the landing, she turned to move towards the West Wing of the mansion. She had always thought the room at the far end, overlooking the fountain, would be a beautiful nursery. She had notebooks full of sketches in the library, of the designs she had imagined for the walls, and of the furniture.

She had, of course, never shown these to Jonathan. Children weren't really on his high priority list. The expedition had taken over his life, and the only gaps left were filled by Marjorie. She opened the door, and was bathed in sunlight, warming her skin, the tears glistening on her face. Her eyes were practically ruby in colour and at this point, her demeanour began to alter, as her bottom lip began to quiver. The white stone that formed the balcony railings, shone in the sun, even with the creeping vines that usually crept along them, dying off for the winter.

Back downstairs, Jonathan and Marjorie had concluded their business and were now reassembling themselves.

"So, you can go six months without that can you?"

Marjorie pulled her dress back up over her shoulders and began buttoning up the clasps at the front.

"I don't think you can. Maybe I should go with you."

She smirked as she looked at Jonathan, now fastening his belt back around his waist.

"I'm sure you would, but this is no place for a woman Marjorie. This is something a man must do. I'm sure you have a bucket list, but mine is much more extreme and honourable."

"Honourable? You just fucked me on your kitchen counter with your wife somewhere in the grounds. Twice. I'm reasonably sure honourable isn't in your vocabulary."

Marjorie's reply seemed to hit a sour note, and Jonathan's face displayed anger. She knew she had misspoken and began to try and retract her statement.

"Jonny, I didn't mean…" she started.

Jonathan strode across towards her and grabbed her by the throat.

"Don't you *ever* speak to me that way again! I fuck you because *I* wish it, not because *you* demand it. Do not forget that this is *my* house. This house was not bought by the deeds of women, and you will remember your place."

He spoke with such antiquated language, maintaining his grip around Marjorie's throat. Sentences like these had not been uttered by men in decades, but Jonathan was a very old soul, and nothing was going to stop him or change him from who he was.

However, Marjorie began to smile, despite his grip on her throat. She altered her gaze down towards Jonathan's erection, and he became disarmed. He released his grip, grabbed Marjorie by the arm and spun her around. He pushed her against the wall, and ripped open the back of her dress, unbuckling his belt once again. Fury bathed his face, now as red as the roses growing outside the window.

However, before a third round of passion could begin, Giles' voice could be heard calling for his master, in a rather panicked tone. Jonathan stopped, and put himself back together, leaving a half-naked Marjorie to try and sort out her own situation as he marched out of the room.

Giles was stood in front of the fountain, staring up at the house when Jonathan joined him.

"Sir, it's your wife. She is on the balcony."

Jonathan looked up, and sure enough, Abigail was standing on the balcony, leaning over the edge. He could see the red in her eyes, and for a moment, felt a small twinge of concern. She looked at him as he moved further towards her.

"Abigail, what are you doing? Stop being ridiculous and get down from there at once."

His commanding voice did nothing to comfort Abigail, or the rest of the house's employees who had now gathered besides Giles, all consumed with worry.

"You know, all I ever wanted was to love you. And to have a family and be happy."

Abigail spoke through a cracked voice, distorted by the well of emotions surging within her. Marjorie emerged from the house, running towards Jonathan, her dress being held together with a safety pin at the front, and a coat draped over her shoulder to cover the evidence of what had gone on in the kitchen.

"I guess you were too interested in fucking young girls and going on your adventures."

Jonathan felt only embarrassment in this moment and showed no concern. The anger which had flowed through him a few moments before with Marjorie was now boiling over. He bellowed across the courtyard, drowning out the flowing water in the fountain.

"ABIGAIL GET THE FUCK DOWN FROM THERE RIGHT NOW!"

Abigail became very calm and very still. She looked down into Jonathan's eyes and smiled. And in that instant, he knew exactly what she was going to do.

"As you wish, darling."

Her motion through the air almost played in slow motion, like a feather falling from height. Marjorie's hand moved to her mouth and Giles and the rest of the staff let out gasps of disbelief.

As Abigail hit the floor, and the blood began to trickle from her head, Jonathan's expression remained the same. He didn't move. He stood there staring at the body of his wife, her eyes still open, the smile still painted onto her face. Jonathan's gaze was drawn to Abigail's right hand.

Within it, was a small emerald, green trinket box that he recognised. It had belonged to Abigail's mother, and she had given it to Abigail as a baby to comfort her when she couldn't sleep. He moved from his position and slowly knelt beside her. He reached for the box, and as he opened it, the box began to play music. As the music played, he noticed a piece of paper in the base. Unfolding the paper, he read what was written on it, and a tear formed in his eye.

'Anthony, or Timothy? Ask Jonathan which name is best for his son.'

The plane shook violently, as the icy winds battered the craft. The windows were now caked in crystals, leaving just enough space between the formations of ice to see the snow streaking past. The plane made a huge shift to the left, as if something has battered the fuselage, and one of the equipment bags came loose, and flew across the interior. As it smashed into the ribs of one of the expedition team, his screams filled the cabin.

Another team member lowered him to the floor and began assessing the injury, while a third attempted to secure all the cargo once again. The pilot and his co-pilot shouted commands at each other, warning buzzers were sounding, and everything in the plane and outside of it were in a state of complete chaos.

But Jonathan just sat there. Still, and silent. He simply stared at the floor, and twirling around in his hands, was the green, emerald music box. In the months since his wife's death, Jonathan had become withdrawn. He no longer presented himself as a Lord, or the owner of a huge mansion, or someone of standing. He had lost weight, now sported a thick white beard, and his eyes were vacant.

He opened the box and re-read the note inside. He had preferred Timothy. His father's name had been Anthony, and he had no intention of following in his mannerism and footsteps. Except he had. His father had abused Jonathan's mother, slept with the maids, controlled every aspect of people's lives, and all in the pursuit of raising his status as much as possible. And now Jonathan had done the same. Abigail hadn't even felt she could come to him and reveal her pregnancy. He was now only committed to the expedition. It was all he had left. He put the box back into his pocket and looked up and out of the window.

The plane had begun it's decent, but it was rough going. Cross winds, and the increasing thickness of the snow were proving to be huge obstacles, and the temperature in the cabin was now a chilling minus-forty-five Celsius. As Jonathan stared out the window, he thought he could make out a figure in the mist, standing on the ice below. He moved to stand up but was thrown back down when the plane hit the ground with an almighty thump, sending all the members of the team cascading down through the cabin, hitting the back wall with force.

The plane bounced back up off the ice and began to tilt to the left.

As Jonathan picked himself back up, the plane hit the ground again, and he rolled down the aisle and into the cockpit, clattering into the pilot, and landing on the controls. The aircraft veered at an angle, the landing gear on the left-hand side collapsed, and the tip of the wing dug into the ice, before breaking away, sending the back end of the plane careering round at speed. The rest of the wing sheared off sending sparks across the frozen surface. The sound of cracks were echoing through the air, and as the remains of the craft slid hard into a snowbank, it split down the middle.

Jonathan watched as three of the team slid through the crack in the middle of the plane and down through the ice into the dark waters now exposed beneath the wreckage. The gap began increasing in size, and the plane groaned in response. Jonathan scrambled out of the cockpit and gathered the remaining three team members. The pilot was trapped in his seat, and the co-pilot had already succumbed to an impact from his head into the control panels, the blood dripping down from his seat.

Jonathan reached back and cut the belt free, and the pilot helped him climb up and out of the door on the right-hand side, now elevated at an angle. The five men gathered on the snow, stood back, and watched, as the plane gradually slipped into the ice, along with their radio and most of their gear. As the tail finally slipped into the water, Jonathan could make out an outline of a person, stood off to the side of the crash site.

It was difficult to see through the mist of the snow and the harshness of the wind, but he was snapped out of his stare by the other team members, who were rushing to gather the gear that had been thrown out of the plane before it was lost to the snow. When he looked back, the figure had gone.

The wind continued to howl outside of the tent, and one of the team, Silvio, was desperately trying to keep the structure pegged into the ice.

"Are you actually going to do something, or just sit there twiddling that fucking box?"

Silvio directed his abuse directly at Jonathan, but it didn't get a response, so he continued reinforcing the anchors as best he could. Jonathan put the box away and reached for a sandwich. He looked at the frozen lump of bread and meat and threw it back down where he found it.

"Hey! That's got to last, don't treat it like a rock!"

Carlos was trying to sift through what had survived, and there was very little food remaining, and even less in the way of drinkable options.

"Why bother, we're going to die anyway. We may as well speed up the process."

Jonathan had had enough of the optimistic approach.

"The plane is gone. The plane that was meant to drop us off, fly back to civilisation, and then return for us. Most of the gear is gone, most of the food is gone, and nobody is expecting us home for six months. Do you really think a fucking sandwich is going to make all the difference?"

"Maybe it will, maybe it won't, but if you don't start trying to help us, I'll speed your death up myself!"

Carlos was the one who had come up with the idea of the expedition in the first place. He wanted to document the wildlife of Antarctica, try and identify new species. But he'd needed the funding, and the Mexican government weren't really interested in looking for penguins and new species of other wildlife, so he went to North America to see Jonathan.

He wanted an adventure. He wanted to chart the entire continent in six months and claim it in the name of the United States and stab a flag in the biggest iceberg he could find. Carlos thought it was all outdated, macho bullshit, but he needed the funding so went along with it.

"You know Carlos, even though I've known you for a long time, I didn't realise how irritating you could be. I think I like it."

Jonathan etched a smile onto his face for the first time in what felt like an eternity. Carlos smiled back, and then continued sorting through the rations.

Jonathan stood and opened the tent doorway and ventured outside. The pilot, and other team member was attempting to set up a second tent to house the supplies, but were not having much luck, as the second tent had a large tear in the side.

"How's it going Archie?" Jonathan asked, as he caught a tent pole that had begun to drift away.

"Not good Jonny, I'm not sure we can patch this with what we have here."

"Any idea if the mayday was transmitted?"

"I managed to send out the signal just before the plane split, and the equipment seemed to still be working, but there's no way to know if it got through the storm."

Icicles began to form in Jonathan's beard, as the moisture in the air froze as soon as it touched any surface. Shielding his eyes from the sharp snow, he looked around for any potential predators, but there appeared to be nothing. But as vision was limited by the icy mist, Jonathan grabbed William, his assistant and they ventured beyond the makeshift camp.

Jonathan armed himself with the only remaining weapon from the gear, a double barrelled shotgun. He knew that unless they were in close quarters, the weapon would be useless against any larger predators, but holding it made him feel more at ease, and reassured William.

Climbing over another bank of snow that had formed against a ridge of ice, William lost his footing, and slipped, rolling into the snow, leaving a man-shaped hole in the blanket of white. Jonathan chuckled to himself and began descending towards William and reached out his hand. But as the wind died down, he stopped in his tracks.

Floating on the wind, appeared to be music. A faint, melody, like a children's trinket box. Instinctively, Jonathan's hand went to his pocket, but there was nothing there. He frantically checked his other pockets, but they were all empty, except for four shotgun shells. The music seemed to get closer, and the wind appeared to die down slightly in response to the notes.

"Do you hear that?" asked Jonathan.

William still sat in his own little hole in the snow strained his ears but replied in the negative.

Jonathan moved past William, and the sound of his protests and headed in the direction of where he thought the music was coming from. Behind him, William managed to pull himself out of the hole, and called Jonathan's name, but he kept walking. The music was now so strong in his ears that he felt as though it was surrounding him. He paused, and looked around, turning three hundred and sixty degrees.

He turned searching in circles so many times at such speed, he fell into the snow, dizzy. When his head stopped spinning, he noticed the music had stopped. And as his eyes focussed, through the snow, he saw the figure in the mist for a third time. Except this time, it wasn't just an outline. Standing above the snow, completely undisturbed by the icy winds, was Abigail.

Jonathan didn't move. He stared at Abigail, and she stared back. Her eyes were cold and icy blue, her lips dark, skin almost as white as the snow. She was wearing the same dress she had worn as she leapt to her death. She smiled at Jonathan, and turned, starting to walk away.

"Wait!" Jonathan called out to her.

She paused and looked over her shoulder at him. She beckoned him with a single finger to follow her, turned away, and continued to move through the mist, without leaving a single footprint in the snow.

"Abigail, please, come back!"

Jonathan was shaken to his very core, but he had a yearning to go after his wife. He stumbled forward through the snow, the wind picking up again, the mist obscuring his vision to the point where he could only just make out Abigail's outline. He called after her again, but she continued her path. The snow was now so thick that Jonathan could barely stand, and with each footstep, seemed to sink further down into it, like it was clambering up his body, trying to claim him.

Finally, he managed to spy Abigail stood approximately ten feet from him, looking back at him, smiling. He smiled back, and a tear formed on his cheek, instantly frozen, and then blown away by the winds. He tried to speak.

"Abigail, I'm so… I'm so sorry. I didn't know."

He pointed to her stomach, and in response, she moved her hand across it, continuing to smile.

"I was a fool. How can you be here? Please, I need you to forgive me."

Jonathan moved closer towards Abigail, stumbling with every step. She didn't move away, waiting for him to get closer. As Jonathan got within touching distance, he reached out his arm, and as he put his foot forward, it met fresh air, and he fell forwards, through Abigail's figure, and plummeted down a massive ice hill, hitting the ice below with such force, he penetrated it, and sank into the icy waters within.

As Jonathan turned in the water, the surface refreezing behind him, he could feel his lungs crystallizing, and his blood freezing, immense pain shattered his senses, and as he sank into the cold dark abyss, he saw Abigail standing on the ice looking down at him, holding the music box, and as he faded into the blackness, he heard the music playing in his head, like a lullaby.

Carlos laid the final bag on the wooden floor in the bedroom, as Marjorie watched on. He turned to look at her.

"Are you okay?" he asked.

"Yes, I'm fine thank you. I'll see that his belongings are sorted and make the arrangements to hand over the property on Wednesday."

She looked at the bags on the floor and wondered whether Jonathan had ever cared for her as much as she had for him. To him, she was just an illicit bit of fun, but to her, he was everything.

"I'd better go, I promised I'd visit William and Silvio in the hospital. They were in a pretty bad way by the time the rescue plane showed up."

Carlos placed a hand on Marjorie's shoulder and left, Giles following him down the corridor and the stairs, the sound of the entrance doors closing echoing around the house.

Marjorie opened the bags and began sorting the clothes from the equipment. She placed the clothes on the dresser, along with a small green, emerald trinket box, and carried the equipment out of the room, and into the hallway. She handed the gear over to Giles, who took it outside, to place in the locker to the rear of the house, and she went into the library to continue the paperwork for the transfer.

Marjorie awoke around eleven-thirty, jolted awake by the lightning illuminating the night sky, and the sound of the rain on the windows. The glass vibrated with the claps of thunder. She closed her notebooks and walked out of the library towards the kitchen. The staff had all retired to their rooms for the night on the other side of the mansion, so she decided to make herself a small sandwich.

As she reached for a knife to cut the bread, she heard the faint sound of music coming from upstairs. She lowered the knife to the marble work surface, and slid between the kitchen doors, attempting to ascertain the source of the music.

"Hello?" she asked into the darkness of the corridor. "Giles? Is that you?"

The music continued, audible above the sound of the rain lashing the windows. As the storm intensified, so did the volume of the music. Marjorie followed the sound to the foot of the stairs, on her way, searching for any musical devices which may have been left on, but found nothing, and in response, began moving up the stairs. The music now surrounded her, and as she reached the landing, she turned towards the West Wing, to see a light on in the bedroom at the end of the hallway.

"That room." Marjorie said aloud to herself. "Of course, it would be that room."

She made her way slowly down the hallway, and the music became almost deafening. Marjorie moved her hands to cover her ears, and as she reached the doorway, it stopped. She investigated the room but saw nobody. There was a dimly lit lantern on a table next to the balcony doors, which were open.

Rain splattered the wooden floor, shining with every flash of lightning. The wind blew the curtains, and they rose like mist into the air, twisting in the harsh breeze. As she moved closer to the doors, the music started again, and as the next flash of lightning lit up the sky, she could see an object on the stone railings outside. The music continued, and when the sky lit up once more, she saw it was the green, emerald music box.

She picked up the lantern from the table and ventured onto the balcony, shielding herself from the rain with her arm. She reached the music box, and picked it up, closing the lid, and ending the music.

Marjorie turned to go back into the house, but as she turned, she was met with the ghostly face of a woman staring back at her. Marjorie screamed, and threw back her arms in fright, as she tumbled over the balcony and fell through the rain to the concrete and stone below. As the stone underneath her began to surge with crimson, above on the balcony, Abigail stood looking down. She walked back into the house, and as Marjorie's eyes closed, she slipped into death listening as Jonathan had, to the lullaby music from the box she still held in her hand.

As her last breath escaped her lips, the music came to an end.

ONE TOO MANY

"Why would anyone want to do a stupid thing like that?"

"Agreed, that's not much of a line from my financial advisor, Kristin, but I was still feeling pretty confident I was doing the right thing."

"Seriously, I mean where is the logic?" Kristin continued.

"Why would you want to buy a 'haunted house' and I use the term very loosely, and then *not* open it as a tourist attraction?"

Kathryn put her hands over her face and leaned forward onto the table as Kristin continued to make her case.

"You have seen *Ghost Adventures*, right? The Haunted Museum? Zak Bagans can afford to buy valuable items and haunted houses that cost millions, and you know why? Because he's a shrewd businessman. So now you have the chance to buy one of the most notorious houses in town, and you just wanna renovate it?"

"It's just gonna be way too much work, and I don't have the kind of commitment for a project like that. I just wanted to renovate it and sell it on," Kathryn protested.

"Yeah, that's what the chick who bought the house with the dolls said, and we all know what happened to her."

"Actually, we don't."

"Just tell me you'll think about it? It's a sound investment, and the bank would back you all the way."

Kathryn knew she wouldn't get any further here, so nodded her head in agreement.

"Okay, fine, I'll think about it."

Kathryn left the offices feeling like she'd been roasted on a spit and served up for the holidays. She knew the house was a great opportunity, but she'd tried projects on this scale before and never seen them through, albeit not in the paranormal area. All those projects had left her with was another level of personal disappointment in her abilities and her conviction.

Kathryn got into her car and headed towards home. She got to the first set of lights, but something was niggling at her. Her home was a left turn, but she turned right and continued on until after ten minutes, she found herself parked outside the murder house. Six women had been murdered in this house over the last five years, and it had taken an intense police operation to apprehend the killer.

John Martin had lived in the house for two years when the first woman went missing. She'd been walking in the park on the way home from her job and been ambushed. They found her body with thirty-two stab wounds in the chest. Martin was captured on CCTV in the park around the same time, although he wasn't captured killing the woman, so the police let him go.

He had been almost non-verbal, and there were even reports of seeing purple flashes in his eyes from the arresting officers. However, at the time, the town was still reeling from the deaths of some children from another notorious house at 1701 Pike Road and so he was released.

Two months later, the bodies of two women were found two streets from the house, both with thirty-two stab wounds in the chest. Again, Martin was a suspect, but with no actual evidence to tie him to the murders, he was never arrested a second time.

Martin finally slipped up when a security camera caught him pull up to the entrance to Santa's Grotto on Christmas Eve as one of the female elves was locking up. He appeared drunk, staggering along the pavement, and walked in front of the camera, and was caught knocking her out from behind. He bundled her into his car and drove her to the house.

The police report said that as he was dragging the woman into the house, two neighbours saw what he was doing, but mistook him for someone trying to help the woman into the house, and they helped him carry her inside. Other witnesses claimed there were flashes of purple light in the windows, but either way, neither neighbour left that house alive.

When the security footage was found, police swooped on the house and Martin was arrested. In the process of linking all the murders together, they discovered carpet fibres from Martin's lounge rug on each of the bodies, meaning he took the bodies home, murdered them in the lounge, cleaned up, and dumped the bodies.

Kathryn parked next to the mailbox, and got out to have a look around, leaving the engine running. The 'For Sale' sign had been replaced by one displaying a 'Sold' plaque. Kathryn had closed the deal on the house a week previously and was now holding the keys. She walked around the property and noticed how creepy the place was. The old, weathered exterior and the natural cobwebs in the windows would help create the perfect atmosphere for a tourist attraction.

Maybe Kristin was right, she should open the place up to the public. She looked through the windows, and saw hundreds of pieces of old furniture, probably belonging to John Martin, left exactly where they were when he was arrested. She'd only been in the house once and hadn't appreciated the commercial aspect of the place until now.

"Maybe I *should* turn this into a business. What have I got to lose?"

Kathryn realised she had been talking to herself, and quickly shut up. She began walking back towards her car, and as she did so, her radio switched to the news. As she began a conversation with an intrigued neighbour who had wandered over for a chat, her radio blurted out an emergency news bulletin.

"Breaking news! Convicted serial killer John Martin is on the loose once again. During a transport to a high security prison, the prison van he was

travelling in was struck by a truck, sending the van into a nearby ravine. Both police officers were killed in the accident, and the back of the van was found empty. Law enforcement officers are asking everyone to be on high alert, and not to approach this man if he is spotted by members of the public. More on this as we get it."

"For the sweet love of Jesus," Kathryn said. "I thought you were on board with this idea. Wasn't it you who came up with it in the first place?"

Kristin sipped her coffee, gesturing her hand in agreement, before responding.

"Yeah, but you didn't tell me you wanted to keep all Martin's furniture."

"Why wouldn't I? That stuff is owned by a serial killer, surely that would attract more visitors. It's guaranteed authentic artefacts."

Kristin sighed and had to concede that Kathryn was right.

"Okay fine, but maybe have a dedicated John Martin exhibition, in the lounge maybe, where the killings took place, and then just put the rest in the attic or something."

Kathryn smiled and interrupted.

"Ah, no I already have an idea for the attic. I'm gonna fill it with creepy dolls. Thought I might try and get my hands on a couple from the Stevenson house."

"1701 Pike? You literally stole my idea from our conversation last week!"

Kristin was irked, but also kinda impressed how closely Kathryn had paid attention. There was something about the way she remembered all the smaller details that always made her smile.

"The only thing is, I need a little help with the renovations. I've already had builders in portioning off some of the rooms to create extra areas, but I could do with help setting up some of the exhibits."

Kristin looked a little shocked. She'd been looking for more excuses to spend time with Kathryn, but manual labour wasn't really one of them.

"So, I have to handle cursed objects, carry them around, and set them all up, and what, go home with a ghost on my shoulder?"

Kathryn smiled and touched her hand.

"I'd really appreciate it if you'd help me with this. It wouldn't have been possible without you."

Kristin looked at her hand beneath Kathryn's and agreed.

Kathryn read the reports with disbelief.

"You mean these guys are serious?" she asked.

"Afraid so, Miss Silverton. They all quit this morning. Claimed they were being pushed in the back, kept hearing moaning coming from the lounge, and when your friend Kristin was arranging the dolls in the attic, one of the guys reckoned the cupboards in the kitchen started slamming on their own."

Kathryn placed her palm to her face as she saw Kristin emerge from the front door.

"Is all this shit true Kristin?" She nodded.

"Yeah, I heard the slamming myself. And I was pretty sure someone was watching me pee when I went to the bathroom. This place is creepier than I thought, and I think we've amped it up by bringing all these objects here. Now I know why Zak Bagans spends most of his time on the road, and not in his museum."

The building foreman continued.

"The good news is the building work itself is complete. The only remaining works left to be done are the interior painting for the kitchen, hallway, and relaying the carpets in the bedrooms where the vampire and pirate exhibits are going. We have a decorating crew coming on Monday, so we should be good to launch on time, but you're gonna need to finish up the exhibits in the completed rooms yourself."

The foreman climbed back into his truck and drove away.

"Kathryn, if you need me to stay and help set things up, I can."

"No, it's okay Kristin, you've done enough. I'll carry on for a few hours tonight, and we can meet up for breakfast in the morning."

"Okay, but hey, make sure you have a cross handy."

Kristin smiled, as she walked down the drive to her car. She waved as she pulled away, and Kathryn went inside, closing the door behind her.

Three days had now gone by. Kathryn had been working non- stop all through Tuesday, Wednesday and Thursday morning. When Kathryn finally paused for a drink and glanced at the clock, it was ten p.m., and three of the four exhibits were set up.

She was excited about what was going into the display she had just finished preparing. As she closed the case which would be housing a pirate medallion, she placed the plaque just inside the door.

Kristin had left on some wild goose chase after she left the house three days ago, to hunt for pirate gold, and called from the airport with the good news that she'd found something. Although she hadn't heard from her since, she knew she was due to fly back in a few days' time. She smiled as she read the plaque she had prepared.

'*This medallion is believed to be twenty-four carat gold. It was found at the supposed location of the wreck of the mythical ship* **Sapphire Serpent***. It is the only piece of treasure to be removed from the wreck due to the reported unforgiving nature of those who still inhabit the ship.*'

Kathryn missed Kristin, and their newfound relationship. She had admired her for a while, but after her last break-up with a previous boyfriend, she had been much more cautious when it came to love. Both her and Kristin were totally invested in this idea, and along with that, everybody loves pirates so failing all else, she'd turn the whole thing into a pirate exhibit. This was exactly the sort of thing that would bring people in.

Suddenly, there was a bang from the attic. Kathryn jumped but put it down to one of the larger dolls falling over and ignored it. She went upstairs to put the doll right, but as she went into the attic, everything was as it should have been. Nothing was out of place, so she assumed she'd heard nothing. As she descended the stairs from the attic onto the landing, she reached the top of the stairs and stopped. The front door was wide open.

"Hello?" she called down the stairs. "Kristin, is that you?" No reply. "Anybody there?"

Another shuffle from in the attic, but Kathryn's attention was drawn to the open door, and she gradually began moving down the main staircase, eyes wide open. There was another noise, this time from behind her, and as she span round, she could've sworn she saw a woman vanish into one of the bedrooms. A cupboard slammed in the kitchen, and Kathryn slipped on a stair near the bottom, and fell the rest of the way.

Scrambling to get up, her ankle burning with pain, she saw another woman move across the kitchen. But it was the sight at the top of the stairs that got her attention. There was a woman standing at the top of the stairs, backed by an eerie blue glow. She was wearing uniform, almost like a fast-food outfit, and Kathryn could see her trying to mouth a word.

She focused in on the woman's lips, ignoring the shuffles going on in the room next to her. Finally, the woman managed to vocalise her word.

"*RUN!*" she shouted at Kathryn and vanished with a scream.

As Kathryn turned on the spot to head out the door, she was met by a fist to the face, issued with full force, sending her flying backwards onto the ground. As John Martin stood over her, blood trickling down from her nose, Kathryn could see the glisten of a blade in the light.

Her legs kicked into overdrive, and she landed a blow to his right shin, and he crumpled. She took the chance to get back to her feet and ran into the kitchen, where the cupboards were going mad. Each door was opening and slamming randomly, the plates inside shattering from the impact. It was then that she saw one of the Stevenson dolls on the counter looking back at her.

Martin appeared in the doorway brandishing his knife, and behind him, Kathryn could make out the blue woman moving towards him.

"*NO!*"

She screamed and launched at him, knocking him into the fridge, sending it over and landing on his chest. He cried out in pain, and

Kathryn stared in disbelief as the doll on the counter turned to face her and pointed to the door. She obliged and ran out, but Martin slashed at her heel with the knife, cutting through the tendon, blood spattering back at his shirt, and Kathryn collapsed to the floor in agony, screaming at the pain as her sock and shoe began to fill with blood.

Martin clambered back to his feet, and staggered forwards, all the time, Kathryn trying to edge her way backwards towards the front door, bathed in excruciating pain. Two women appeared directly in front of Martin and collectively picked him up and threw him backwards smashing through the grandfather clock in the hallway and sending debris crashing to the floor. His leg became impaled by a piece of mahogany wood, right through his thigh.

He moaned in pain, but the voice seemed deeper than one would expect. As he looked back towards Kathryn, his eyes flashed purple, and in a building rage, he gripped the wood fragment and ripped it out, causing him to scream again, and blood to trickle from his wound.

Kathryn had reached the front door, but now found it had been locked somehow, and began shuffling backwards up the stairs, leaving a blood trail behind her, which was becoming increasingly heavier. Martin staggered forwards, and gripped the banister, hauling himself up the stairs towards Kathryn.

He reached her functioning leg, and grabbed hold, dragging her back down in front of him, and he raised his knife and plunged it into her side, audibly grazing bone and it did so. Kathryn screamed so loud; it nearly shattered the nearby glass display cases. As Martin extracted the dagger from her side and prepared for another blow, the blue woman flew down the stairs sending him flying backwards through the air, and he landed flat on his back on the hallway floor, smacking his head on the hard wooden surface, with a loud crack.

Tears now streaked Kathryn's face as she held her hands to her side. The blood continued to seep through her shirt, her leg was now numb with her shoe oozing blood, and she began feeling very lightheaded. She knew it was only a matter of time before she passed out as the adrenaline started to wear off, and as she looked back at Martin's crumpled body, she could see him stirring, his knife just three feet away.

From behind her came the sound of footsteps, and she felt herself becoming lighter. Believing to finally be losing consciousness, she felt a floating sensation, and it seemed almost as if she was flying above John Martin lying on the floor. She landed with a thump, jolting both knife wounds, but found herself next to the knife itself. Was she hallucinating, or was this real?

Kathryn found some inner strength and decided either way, she wasn't going down without a fight. She reached forward and grabbed hold of the knife, but her hand was slammed back down to the ground as Martin grabbed hold of it too. She looked up and he smacked her across the face, sending her back onto the floor. He picked up the blade and began climbing to his feet.

Kathryn slid her way into the lounge and found herself on the very carpet all the women before her had been murdered on. This was it. She was going to be the seventh victim of John Martin in his house. He stood above her, raising the knife, and brought the blade plunging down.

Kathryn closed her eyes, waiting for the inevitable, but nothing came. She opened her eyes, and saw Martin's arm frozen in the air, surrounded by a blue glow. As she opened her eyes fully, and focused on the image unfolding before her, she saw six women surrounding John Martin. The blue woman was holding onto his arm, two others were pulling him from behind, another two each had hold of a leg, and the sixth took the knife from his hand. She glanced over her transparent shoulder at Kathryn, and smiled reassuringly, before turning back to face John Martin.

"No more women. This is one too many."

The woman plunged the knife into Martin's heart, his eyes bulging, still held back by the spirits of the five women he'd killed, with the sixth somehow repeatedly plunging the blade into his chest. When the thirty-second wound had been created, the woman dropped the blade, and the others released their grip on Martin, and he fell to the floor in a bloody heap. A spiral of dark mauve coloured smoke slowly filtered out of John Martin's mouth, but before she could process what was happening, the adrenaline finally vanished.

As Kathryn lost consciousness, she felt the cool night air on her face, and the soft grass beneath her.

"It was all so surreal. It was like they were protecting me. I mean, I needed it, as I found out, I wasn't prepared for an attack by an escaped serial killer."

The group laughed, and some took pictures of the display case and its contents.

"But you guys know the rest, and if you don't, visit the gift shop where you can get your hands on an unabridged version of what happened."

Kathryn directed the group into the next room. She paused briefly to glance at the knife in the case behind her. She didn't know if the purple smoke has been real, or if it was her consciousness letting go, but it still plagued her mind. Kristin was on her way back with pirate treasure and the museum had started with quite a bang.

The knife in the case still had the blood of John Martin on the handle. Kathryn smiled to herself and followed the group towards the pirate room.

As they all left, a sound of vibration could be heard. As the tour group rounded the corner, in the display case, the knife began to move.

LIFE AFTER LIFE

Some people say that life after death is a religious thing, or something you only see on TV. Some people believe that there is a heaven and a hell, and others believe that there is nothing but darkness, and there is no existence after death. And if people could ask me what life after death is like, I would say one thing. Boring.

When you're trapped in the same place for day after day for hundreds of years, you find it difficult to find the positives. I know every inch of this house, every piece of history since it's construction, and I know everybody else who lives here.

Everyone, and everything. That's right, not every consciousness dwelling here is human. Or was human. It's really one for the religious nuts to figure out.

There are fifteen of us living here. Most of us keep to ourselves, but every so often we get visitors, and that's when it's fun to really interact. When you're dead for as long as I've been, you find ways to amuse yourself. Moving objects, opening doors, whispering into somebody's ear. You know, just messing around.

The best way for me to describe this place is kinda like a school yard. There are the nerdy kids, the ones who stay in the rooms where they died just contemplating their existence, and then there are the bullies. In this case, the resident demons. I was quite lucky. I died of natural causes. Christine who lives upstairs in the attic, she was murdered up there by a jealous kid who just couldn't accept that she wasn't interested in him. He'd tried to get around it by offering to tutor her, but when he tried to kiss her and she slapped him back, he lost his shit and hit her in the face with a bronze statue. And that's where they found her.

I heard from the priest apparition next door that they found the kid's body down the street a week later. Christine was thrilled. You would be too if you'd spent two weeks sitting in the attic watching your own body decompose because, and I quote, 'some geeky little freak', couldn't get his leg over.

Alison is another curious case. She is the only one in the house to have been killed outside of the house. She didn't even live here, so nobody was quite sure how she got here. She likes to wander the halls, just up and down, all day and then at night, she sits on top of the kitchen table. When she arrived, I remember being a bit confused because I've watched over all the people come and go in this house, and then tried to welcome them as they passed into our realm, but I'd never seen her before.

As it turned out, she had been a victim of a demonic possession right across town, and when the demon latched on to the person who bought this house, somehow, it carried her with him.

There was a whole cleansing thing, and she was left here. She doesn't talk much since the demon was banished. It's almost like she became that attached to it, that she doesn't know what to do with herself anymore.

I should explain something. The spirits and the demons don't interact. We aren't *able* to interact as you would call it.

People assume there are three levels to this whole life and death thing. First you live, then you die but remain as a spirit in some other worldly realm, and then you crossover to heaven or whatever. That isn't the case. It's much more scientific than that. When we die, or at least in our personal experiences here, our soul or consciousness leaves the body, and we just wake up one day to find we are where we left off.

Except we're dead.

So, we exist in your realm just as much as we did before, we're just in a kind of phased existence. Demons however, live in a totally different plain. They come along whenever there is a violent death or a action, to attempt to consume what's left of that energy, and then they go back to the dimension they come from. Unless of course some ghost hunting geeks decide to try and summon them.

They hate that.

Imagine you're asleep in bed at like two in the morning, and someone drags you out of bed by your ankles and floats you above a table. You wouldn't like it either.

Speaking of ghost hunting nerdlings, they are my favourite distraction. There has been so much death and violence in this house that there are a lot of us to try and keep busy, which means we cause a lot of what they call 'Paranormal Activity' and that means the house garnered a reputation for ghosts and then every couple of years, we get a new group of investigators, convinced that they are going to be the ones to become famous and prove the existence of ghosts.

Ghosts don't cross over to heaven or hell. Eventually, our energy diminishes after maybe a thousand years, and we cease to be. This is sped up by things like exorcisms or blessings, but there isn't a higher plain for us. Some spirits can attach themselves to someone they loved rather than where they died, but that's usually because the telepathic desire from the person left behind is so strong that it acts like a tether.

That happened for my sister Natalie. My parents always preferred her to me, as I was always the one to cause trouble, and she was the perfect daughter. I think that's why when she died, I never saw her here until my parents moved out and I caught her walking down the front path with them, and she looked back at smiled at me.

Last week, was undoubtedly my favourite group of ghost hunters yet. Imagine a group of extreme tech nerds who spend four hours a day in the gym, so people take them more seriously, but deep down they are still super nerds. Yeah, you've got the image. Well, they decided to interview the caretaker of the house, and I'd spent the last six years trying to perfect turning the lights on and off, so I was eager to test it on some actual victims.

I watched them enter the front door, looking like some army- reject *Ghostbusters*. I may have died four-hundred years ago, but I do watch

TV. They sat down in the lounge with Steve, and immediately got their crew to close all the curtains and set up some red lighting, you know, because a genuinely haunted house isn't creepy enough for TV. When the interview started, that's when I decided it was my time to shine.

"So, Steve, tell me about the experiences that go on in this house."

I mean, the guy could not have put more dramatic tone into one sentence if he tried.

"Well, we have all sorts of activity going on in here. I've been pushed in the basement, and I've seen a ghostly white figure at the end of the first-floor hallway," replied Steve.

I did my best not to laugh at the fact that Steve had never actually gone into the basement and was lying through his teeth. Mainly because he was a serious wimp, but mainly because I kept locking the door and hiding the key. And as for the ghostly white figure, none of us here wear white. I myself sport a spiffy blue ensemble. But the interview continued.

"You've been pushed? Like, physically pushed?"

Very eager investigator man was now becoming increasingly wide eyed. Whether that was for the camera, or genuine, I couldn't tell, but I knew this was going to be fun.

"Yeah, I went down there to check on some damp we had been trying to deal with, and I heard a shuffling in the far corner under the window. When I went over there to take a look, I felt a pair of hands on my chest, and I got shoved right back and landed on my ass. I tell you, I got right up and ran out of there, and I swear I could hear laughing."

There was a definite sound of laughing, but it was coming from me.

"Did you hear that?"

Investigator man was very on edge. His head perked up like a meerkat.

"I just heard a little girl laughing."

Little girl? I'm sixteen thank you very much.

"Dude, I heard that too!" exclaimed the camera operator.

What is it with men, excitement and the word 'dude'. First lesson of ghost investigation, and their most used words. Number one is 'dude'. Number two is 'bro' and number three is 'right' but posed in question format.

"Bro, I need you to go grab that digital recorder right now."

And there it is. First 'bro' of the day. Now I choose not to communicate through digital recorders, because often, what I say is never what they hear. I'll give you an example. Excited camera man handed investigator man a recorder, and started asking questions, before reviewing it live.

"Who is here with us right now?" "*Laurie.*"

"OH MY GOD BRO! DID YOU HEAR THAT? IT SAID THE DEVIL!"

I did not say the devil was here, I literally just said my name.

"Often spirits or demons take on the manifestation or the sound of little kids to trick you into a false sense of security," he explained to Steve, who was clearly shitting his pants but wanted his fifteen minutes of fame.

He nodded his head and stayed still. Camera guy was darting back and forth with his upper body, but his feet were fixed to the ground. They reviewed more of the questions they asked me.

"Are you really the Devil, or are you a little girl spirit that is trapped here? How many spirits are here with us right now?"

"*I'm not the Devil, and I'm sixteen.*"

"OH MY GOD DUDE, IT SAID I'M THE DEVIL, AND THERE'S SIXTEEN SPIRITS HERE!"

For the love of God. Why do I bother. Although to be fair, sixteen spirits was only one off. The final question was a doozy.

"Can you do something to show us that you're here right now?"

My time to sparkle. Not literally of course. I concentrated, reached out my hand, and hit the switch.

"DUDE! THE LIGHTS JUST WENT OUT!" "ARE YOU SERIOUS RIGHT NOW BRO?"

"I asked it to show us it was here right now, and it totally flicked the lights out!"

"AND I HEAR THE LAUGHING AGAIN!"

I just couldn't help it, the excitement and over emphasising these guys were doing was just too laughable. I get the fact they are here to capture evidence of spirits, and I'm happy to give it to them, even if they interpret it wrong, but they get so over excited, I can't help myself.

I reached out and switched the lights back on, and then they truly lost their minds. The next twenty minutes was them trying to figure out which equipment they would use first. Personally, I prefer the Ovilus devices. I like to randomly confuse them and then watch them interpret what I said in a completely invented way.

"We need to investigate this house, right now. We aren't waiting for tomorrow; this is way too much activity to wait."

Steve seemed disappointed by this, as I think he was hoping for a little more airtime, but he agreed and planned for them to set up their cameras and stuff, and I went back upstairs, waving at Harold, the resident pensioner spirit, as I headed up to the attic to chat with Christine.

"So, what are these guys like?" Christine asked me.

"Probably the most intense bunch we've had. So, I wanna mess with them on as many devices as possible."

"Are we talking throwing objects, or physical appearances?"

She seemed quite excited for a break in our routine. After all, only a couple of us could freely move around the house. The others were bound to their rooms.

"I wanna save the apparition part until the end of the night, and I think we should get Francis to do it."

Christine laughed her head off at the thought of a naked elderly man floating in front of the living.

"If they see that, then they'll probably end up adding to our numbers, because they're gonna have a heart attack!"

She laughed loudly again, and from downstairs I could just make out the camera guy's voice.

"Dude? Did you hear that? Sounded like the little girl again!" "See what I mean?" I asked.

"Okay, I'll tell Francis, but I'm not gonna get that image out of my head for the next two centuries, so next time, you're talking to him!"

"Deal."

"Okay, so we are here in the famous Highland Manor house, and we have already seen a huge amount of activity since we got here. We have heard laughter of a little girl, we have captured EVP of someone saying they are the Devil, and that there are sixteen spirits here. We've also had lights go on and off, and reports of the caretaker being pushed in the basement. Now it's time to lock the doors and investigate this fascinating house. Okay cut, how was that?"

As suspected, the whole dramatized effect of his words, were purely for the camera. I was relatively sure he didn't believe what Steve had told him. Probably because they walked around the house and found that there were no basement windows for the ghosts to hide under.

"Okay roll again, and I'll flesh out the intro a little."

"Yeah, so go over the history of the house a little more, I don't think we spooked it up enough."

"Right? I knew I should've gone more dramatic!" And there was most used word number three. "Okay rolling and go."

"This house has seen multiple murders, suicides, and even demonic activity. It is located just two blocks from the infamous 1701 Pike Road, and only three blocks from the new Haunted Museum. This is a house of death, and despair. It comes to claim the living and terrorise those who enter its doors and roam its hallways. But we're gonna stop them. We are going to banish the evil in this house, to help the owners who are now beside themselves with fear. This… is Highland Manor."

"Okay, so we have static night vision cameras on each of the three floors, and one in the attic. The caretaker Steve gave us the key to the basement. A key, which he reports, likes to mysteriously vanish. It is almost like someone doesn't want him down there. We wanna know why. And that is where we are going to start our investigation."

Investigator man made quite an effort of unlocking the door, and I'm pretty sure that it wasn't deliberately dramatic. I just think he was a bit dumb and couldn't get the thing in the hole. Something I suspected haunted the rest of his life too.

There were five in this team of intrepid explorers. I learnt the Investigator man was called John, and the camera guy was called Hector. The other three were just referred to as Wes, Will and Frank. I had no idea who was who, but I was more focussed on the task at hand. It had been seven years since the last team had come, and while that wasn't an eternity when you're basically immortal, it had been a long gap between chances for fun.

I followed John down the stairs, and moved to stand between him and Hector, which stopped them dead. Stage One, freeze them out of their comfort zone.

"Dude, it just got ice cold right here. FEEL THIS BRO!"

I was beginning to love the ease of provoking Hector, he seemed to be even more excitable than John. If only they could see that they were running their hands through the body of a sixteen-year-old girl. I tried not to giggle at the horror. I didn't want to peak too early. I moved away, and as I passed John, I ran my hand down his arm, and moved over to sit on the dryer against the far wall.

"John, I just saw a ball of light move out of your back and then head over to the left."

Wes, just a guess by the way, still no idea who was who, was now staring into his camera's display screen and was reviewing the tiny speck of light he'd caught as I'd moved away. Ghost hunters think that it's manifestation or a representation of a spirit, but in actual fact, it's just a brief moment where our two worlds are visible to each other, usually due to some heightened brain activity or some electrical presence.

I suspected it was because they were so overexcited. They were looking at my fingernail, but I didn't want to rain on their parade, so I carried on with the plan.

"Hector, hand me the spirit box."

John was now moving to the only thing I hate more than the digital recorder, the spirit box. There is so much static that they never hear what is being said. With the last group, they had asked how I died, and I responded with natural causes. But they heard the phrase 'waterboarded' and presumed I'd been tortured to death.

The static sweep began, and I moved back towards them to give as accurate a response as possible. I always tried to be genuine before I began messing with people.

"What is your name?"

"My name is Laurie."

"Harry! I heard Harry!"

"Oh, for God's sake."

"OH MY GOD DUDE! It said your life is at stake!"

I kept quiet and waited for the next question.

"Why do you remain here? What is your purpose in this house?"

"I live here, what are you doing in this house?"

"Bro, I swear I just heard a full sentence. That had definite vocal tone. Let's try another one. How did you die?"

Here we go. I got as close to the spirit box as I possibly could and spoke very clearly.

"Natural… Causes."

"DUDE! HE SAID HE WAS WATERBOARDED!"

I held my head in my hands. I was so done with this session. I went and sat on the dryer with a thud.

"Hey, did you guys hear that?" Will asked.

John turned off the noise of the box and they all stood there staring at me. For a minute I thought they could see me. They looked like scared statues. I jumped down from the dryer and picked up a screw that was lying on the floor. Still, they stared at me, trying to see through the darkness. I threw the screw at the staircase, and it landed with a very quiet sound, and rolled back down the stairs.

They all lost it.

"OH MY GOD DUDE, SOMETHING JUST LANDED RIGHT BESIDE ME!"

"JOHN DID YOU SEE THAT!"

"WES GET OVER HERE RIGHT NOW, DOCUMENT THIS!"

They must have spent at least ten minutes trying to find this screw, before telling the camera that it could not be debunked, and they moved back upstairs.

"After our intense flurry of activity in the basement, we decided to leave Harry alone, and move back up to the main floor."

Harry. We only have three males here, and none of them are called

Harry. How do you even get Harry from Laurie? I got so irritated, I accidentally made one of their static cameras shut off.

I tend to drain battery power when I get annoyed. Acts kind of like a magnet, and then I calm down and I feel better. This provided the crew with much confusion, but they were determined to 'document' this evidence, because you know, batteries never run out. Obviously.

"Okay, we are now moving up to the first floor, this is where Steve told us he saw a ghostly white figure at the end of the hallway, so we have a night vision camera focused down there, we have Wes taking still photos with the full spectrum camera, and we are going to try using the Structured Light Sensor camera to detect any figures that may be up here."

Now, the SLS is my personal favourite camera, because they do indeed pick up our forms. However, the infrared can cause minor pain to us spirits, so we tend not to stay in shot for too long. The light drains our energy, so we usually make ourselves known, act a few moves out and then step out of the limelight.

Hector was aiming the SLS at my bedroom, so naturally I slipped inside, and sat on the bed. Now these cameras don't pick us up until we move, so I sat perfectly still, waiting for their first request.

"Okay spirits. We've met Harry downstairs already, so we know you're here, but we wanna meet more of you. Can you show yourself to us?"

Sorry Hector, too vague. If you want my attention, make a more outrageous request.

"Are there dark entities here?"

Nearly, but not quite enough. Let John have a go.

"Can you show us how you died?"

Christine was stood behind them in the doorway giggling. We'd done this before. She nodded, and I sprang to action.

"DUDE! I'VE GOT A FIGURE RIGHT NEXT TO THE BED!"

Hector was so animated he nearly dropped the damn thing. I was chuckling to myself as I put my hands round my throat and mimicked being strangled. There was a slight tingling in my chest but not enough to stop just yet.

"What is it doing? It looks like it's pointing to the ceiling." "What are you pointing at?" asked John.

I wasn't pointing at anything, so I stopped my drama act. I looked at Christine, and she nodded and entered the room.

"Dude, it just went so cold here, I've got full body chills. And now they're gone. No wait, they're back and… OH MY GOD THERE'S ANOTHER FIGURE!"

This was just too hilarious. Christine was doing a full-on Egyptian dance on top of the bed.

"Bro, it looks like it's pointing at the first figure! Like it's trying to touch it on the arm!"

"Hey that's exactly where I just felt the cold spot, right on my arm."

John looked directly at the camera.

"Could this be the spirit trying to tell Will that it just touched him on his arm?"

The tingling got too much for me, so I rapidly collapsed on the floor, and my figure dropped off the map.

"Woah John, the first figure's gone."

Christine started throwing her hands in the air as she jumped up and down.

"Hey, it's pointing to the ceiling just like the other figure!" "Are you pointing to something?"

Christine got fed up and stepped off the bed, and then collapsed onto the floor right next to me, and we waited.

"OH MY GOD! IT JUST JUMPED THROUGH THE WALL!"

"That was totally awesome!"

"Oh hey, you know what? There was a girl who died in the attic, and the figure kept pointing upwards," said Wes/Will.

"That's right! Let's head up there now."

It was at this point that I noticed the third of the background trio wasn't around. Where was Frank? Then one of the guys radioed him.

"Hey Frank, we're moving up to the attic, any unusual activity up there?"

"No guys, nothing yet, just a few noises but that could be a rat or something."

As the guys moved out of the room, me and Christine stood up and as they rounded the corner, from the opposite corner, Celia, another of our residents, appeared in the doorway.

"More ghost obsessed losers?" she asked.

"Yeah," I replied, "but these ones are extra obsessed."

"Well, make sure they don't disturb Julius. He's in a real bad mood tonight. Steve knocked his ashes over this morning and vacuumed them up and left them in there."

"I'm pretty sure they're heading for the attic, but we will try and keep them away from him."

Christine ran ahead, and up the stairs to the second floor to prepare to scare them away from Julius. He was one of the few original inhabitants who had a presence here. He'd been the original owner's son who died of a broken heart when his lover left him. His father had him cremated and placed on the fireplace in the lounge, and then found love with the same woman, and left the house, leaving Julius behind. Not that he was bitter about it or anything.

Having popped by the command centre in the kitchen to slam a door and scare the living daylights out of Frank, I ran up to the second floor, where unfortunately, the scaring tactic hadn't worked, and I just saw Julius shouting at John, and Christine trying to calm him down. He was shouting into their spirit box so loudly, that all they could hear was static, and the occasional 'calm down' from Christine. The fact they couldn't hear him only made him angrier, and the angrier he got, the darker the hallway felt. I could tell something was coming, so I tried to drag Julius away from the team.

"Julius, you need to calm down or it's going to come back."

"I DO NOT CARE WHAT COMES BACK! THESE PEOPLE HAVE NO RIGHT TO DISTURB MY REST! THIS IS MY HOME AND THEY MUST LEAVE!"

"OH MY GOD DUDE! IT JUST SHOUTED 'LEAVE'!"

Upon registering they had finally heard him, Julius began to calm down, but it was too late. The hallway got darker, and I could feel the heaviness in the air.

"We need to go, now." I pulled Julius and Christine into the nearest room, and we huddled down in the corner. From outside the doorway, we could hear the guys musing.

"I swear the air just got super heavy, and I have this nervous, intense feeling," said Hector.

"Guys, my camera just shut off," said Will/Wes. "Are you serious?" asked John.

I called to them from the bedroom, thinking they would hear me, because what had entered the house was not good.

"Hey guys, you'd better get out of there. Just run!"

That, they heard.

"Dude! It just said RUN!"

Hector was now very animated, but they didn't move. "Aww man, I don't feel good right now."

"What's wrong Hector?" asked John.

"I just feel all this rage inside me. I wanna just, like, attack you dude. I'm not even kidding right now."

We watched the black shadow move past the doorway towards Hector. We knew what was coming. And Julius was very aware that he had brought it back.

"I'm sorry, I'm sorry, I'm sorry, please, I'm sorry." He kept saying it repeatedly.

Out in the hall, things were getting more intense.

"Hey John, this thing just said sorry over and over again." Hector lost it.

"I don't care, just get out of my face dude!"

He punched the static camera and it crashed to the floor, and he smacked the spirit box out of Wes/Will's hand, and it rolled into the room where we were hiding.

"I gotta get out of here."

Hector headed downstairs… with the demon on his back.

"Okay, so we are about to wrap up this investigation. Hector has had to leave the house, he is showing some worrying signs of an oppression, so Wes, and myself, are going to head up to the attic to try and communicate with the girl who died up there. We are going to use the

Paranormal Puck 2 device, which allows the spirits to manipulate environmental conditions to choose words from a database and respond directly to our questions. Ready? Let's go."

Christine and I were sat in the window waiting. Julius had shut himself in his room, now terrified that he might be responsible for bringing the dark energy back to the house. The fun had now gone from the situation. We had not had a demon enter the house for over fifty years. The last time, it took one of us with it.

Attached to a human, it could kill them.

It was important to try and let the team know. John and Wes sat directly opposite us while Will placed the puck in the centre of the room. I hadn't seen this device before, but it seemed like the Ovilus so I was pretty sure I could communicate with it.

They began asking questions.

"Is there anybody here with us?"

I concentrated and began to answer.

"*Yes.*"

The device picked up on my exact word. This seemed to delight the trio immensely.

"How many spirits are here with us right now?"

"*Two.*"

"Two? Okay that's good, hello. What are the names of those here with us?"

"*Laurie. Christine.*"

"Hi Laurie, hi Christine. Can you tell us how you died?"

They were running out of time; it was time to shift the focus.

"*Hector. Danger.*"

"OH MY GOD DUDE, IT SAID HECTOR, DANGER!"

John started freaking out. I needed them to listen, to understand.

"Why is Hector in danger?" asked John.

"*Demon. Back. Malicious.*"

"DEMON! MALICIOUS!"

"Bro, this thing is going off! Where is Hector?"

"He's outside, but he's fine. Does Hector have a demon attachment? Is that why he's so angry right now?"

"*Yes. Help. Cleansing.*"

"Man, this is creeping me out right now! What will happen if we don't cleanse Hector?"

I concentrated as hard as I could and sent a series of words through the device.

"Death. Spirits. Deceased. Help. Please."

I fell to the floor, exhausted, as the men tried to grasp what I had communicated with them. But they started cheering and high fiving each other, ecstatic with the evidence they had captured. They did not seem convinced of helping Hector at all. Christine tried to get through to them.

"Hector. Save. Must. Demon. Kill."

"Dude, it just said demon must kill! That's awesome!"

As they wrapped up the equipment, and began carrying it out of the building, an exhausted Christine and I lay on the ledge looking out of the window. As all the cameras and devices were locked away and the team got into the van, Hector stopped. He turned around and looked up directly at us, smiled, and got into the van.

As much as I love winding visitors up, and Steve of course, some of them take it too far. That was proven that night.

Between us planning to scare them with tricks and funny responses and the very real threat of death, they failed to understand the severity of their actions.

Hector now lives in the second-floor bathroom. He wanders down the hallway from time to time, but he is still trying to come to terms with what he is now. All I can say is that it's a good job Francis didn't wake up to perform his trick, or we'd have more than just one new addition to the family.

THE CRACKS BETWEEN

Antique shops can be grim places for a ten-year-old. Full of things they've never heard of, covered in dust, and with that unique old-person musk that lingers on the objects almost like the dust itself. You inhale the unique aroma and instantly think of Werther's Originals.

But for Annie, this was a place of wonder. Things from fairy tales and episodes of *Goosebumps*. Any object could magically transport you to a different time and place, and you could let your imagination run wild. And of course, what else are you meant to do when you're ten these days, other than stare blankly at a six-inch screen scrolling through videos of morons hurting themselves doing stupid stunts on the internet.

Annie wasn't like most ten-year-old girls. She wasn't like most people. Her mother had always told her that she had an 'old soul', and she was born in the wrong time. She had a fascination with old books, the pages yellowed with age and the hardback covers worn over time. There was no better place to come for old hardback books full of intrigue than Herman's Curiosities.

Old man Herman seemed to have an endless supply of books. Every time her father purchased one for Annie, another one would appear in its place as if by magic. Arthur, her father, told Annie tales of her mother coming to the store when she too was

a child. He claimed that she must be channelling her mother somehow. That of course was no bad thing. Annie's mother had been lost when she was just five, but her memories were strong. It was almost like she had never left her side.

"Daddy, can I have this one please? It's so beautiful."

Annie had picked out a large leather-bound volume, at least eight-hundred pages thick. Pages which were gold edged, and the cover was made with a relief of an even more golden elephant, with two silver embossed stone pillars either side.

The book was entitled 'Ancient African Myths'.

Arthur smiled down at his daughter, and he could see Herman smiling at the counter too.

"Oh, I'm not sure, Angel, you'd better ask Mr Fredericks," Arthur said as he shot Herman a wink.

Annie clutched the book excitedly to her chest and ran up to the dusty glass counter and pushed the book above her head and on to the top.

"Excuse me Mr Fredericks, please may I have this book? I have the monies."

Herman Fredericks was a kind old soul, and he knew that Annie was probably the only person who ever actually bought any of the books, most of which he doesn't even remember stocking. He always played a little game with Annie and her father played along.

"Well Miss Annie, I'm sure I could let it go but it's going to cost you a pretty penny."

Annie pulled a little *Teletubbies* coin purse out from her coat pocket and opened it up. She placed its entire contents onto the counter. Herman looked down at eight individual pennies, three buttons, and a safety pin. He stifled a grin and rubbed his little beard as he so often did when he play acted with Annie.

"I suppose that I could let it go for this much, save some pennies for next time Miss Annie."

Herman slid four pennies away, and a button, and scooped the rest back into Annie's purse, before secretly popping the rest back in before closing it, glancing over at her father, who smiled in response. A very excited Annie grabbed the book, gave Herman a little wave and ran back towards the entrance to the store.

Arthur slid up to Herman, who held up five fingers, and Arthur slid a note across the glass, and waved goodbye as he followed his daughter out of the door. Arthur closed the door behind them, jingling the typical store bell above the door, but as Herman turned to place the money in the till, he heard the bell jingle again.

He turned to greet the next customer, but there was nobody there. Blaming the wind, he walked around the counter to shut the door, but as he got halfway to the open doorway, it began to rattle and vibrate. As fast as it had opened, it slammed shut, snapping the bracket, and sending the bell crashing to the floor.

Herman was incredibly startled, and jumped at the noise of the door, taking a massive deep breath. He held his chest, his heart pounding, and moved back to sit behind the counter on his sturdy nineteen-hundreds stool. As he sat down, still calming himself, he glanced over at the bell still on the floor.

Sighing that he hadn't picked it up, he stood up once more. As he did so, the bell began to move. Slowly at first, but then quicker, like it was being dragged by an unseen force. Herman stopped in his tracks, and his eyes became wide, and his heart pounded quicker, as the bell moved closer and closer to him.

He tried to move backwards, but bumped into one of the solid pine bookcases, and as the bell reached his feet, it went between his legs, and continued on, but something shot through him, like an outlined gust of wind. It hit him full force, and his chest exploded with pain from within. Moments before he hit the ground, he could see what looked like an old cart pull up outside the store, but the street seemed different, emptier. As Herman faded into sleep, he heard a whisper of a voice.

"Stop kicking that bell Annie and just pick it up."

"You know, Dad, these are the best books I've ever read. I mean when was the last time you saw this fascinating a collection? Nobody has these anymore, they're just dicking about on iPads and smartphones. Sometimes I think I'm the last person alive under twenty who owns a real book."

Annie walked around the store, taking in the memories. It had been at least seven years since she was last in here. She thought of old Mr Fredericks, and a little note of pain flowed through her heart.

"I think you're probably right Angel. No appreciation for anything anymore, that's the problem with the youth of today."

"Spoken like a true old man!"

Arthur winced at the thought of him being classed as an old man. When he was younger, fifty wasn't old, it was a man's prime. Times had changed though. The street was evidence of that. In the seven years since they'd last been here, three coffee shops and a vape store had opened opposite.

The only thing that hadn't changed at all was Herman's Curiosities. Being closed for five years will have that effect, of course, but Arthur was staggered at how little the store had cost.

"You know, you don't get to ask me for any books now you own a store, young lady. You should be buying me things."

Annie turned and smiled at him.

"You know this store doesn't make any money. It's about the intrigue and the history, and the stories that come with these objects. You can't put a price on that, Dad."

"Maybe that's why nobody wanted to pay for it. When even *Starbucks* decide to build a new store opposite rather than convert this one, you know something must be wrong with it."

"You know, anyone else these days who paid fifteen grand for a building would be jumping with joy at the prospects."

"Yeah, but you're not bothered about the prospects, you just want to sit here all day reading your books, looking at your antiques. Wouldn't hurt you to have a little cafe up the corner over there, at least you'd make a little money. You know, I wouldn't mind one of those *Xbox Series X* consoles your uncle keeps going on about."

Annie gave him one of those 'you'll be lucky' looks and carried on looking around. She thought of what must have happened to old Mr Fredericks. They never did find him. She always thought he'd taken retirement, and simply left town.

The people who lived nearby said he never left the store, and always said he'd probably end up dying there. A part of Annie was slightly worried she'd see his body behind a bookcase somewhere. Shrugging off that negative image, she wandered between those very bookcases, and stopped when she saw something.

As she glanced towards the section labelled 'Mythology', she saw a gap on the shelf. As she got closer, she realised what it was. The gap was from the last book she had bought from here. *Ancient African Mythology* had sat in that very space on the shelf. Dust had now gathered there, but there was no doubt.

She touched the shelf with her hand, and as she did so, a noise came from behind her, almost like the sound of a book hitting the floor.

"Dad was that you?" she asked.

"No honey, I'm talking to the neighbours," came the reply.

Annie could indeed hear voices from the entrance. Arthur did like to make friends anywhere and anytime. People were probably curious as to what was going on. She vaguely heard the question, "Did they ever find his body?", before moving away to investigate the noise she heard.

She moved to the other side of the bookcase, and there on the floor, open on the carpet, was indeed a book.

"I must have knocked it off from the other side," she said aloud to herself.

She walked towards it to pick it up but stopped dead when she saw the page turn. The sound of faded giggling could be heard from where the book was sat, and as she watched, the pages turned again. Frozen to the spot, Annie tried to call for her father, but the words wouldn't come out, and as the pages turned for a third time, she swore she could almost make out the outline of a figure, lying on the floor.

"What are you looking for, angel?"

Her father appeared behind her and startled her to the point where she leapt off the floor.

"Jesus Dad! Don't creep up on me like that!"

As she spun back around, the book was gone. Nothing out of place, no figure, no giggling.

"Sorry, what were you staring at?"

Annie looked back at where the book had been positioned and turned back to her father.

"Nothing, don't worry about it."

The lights in the store weren't very bright, and the moonlight seemed to be brighter than the light bulbs. Annie had spent most of the day reading through the inventories of what Herman had in the store when he disappeared.

Arthur had left several hours before to meet her uncle to test out his 'new-fangled gaming machine' but she had decided to stay. Her eyes began to droop, and she glanced up at the *Starbucks* opposite, and decided she could do with a caffeine injection. She got up from the stool, and walked out the door, the night air soothing to her skin after being in the hot stuffy store all day. She locked the door and crossed the street to get her fix.

As the white chocolate mocha with blonde espresso roast slid down her throat, (her favourite) she could feel the coffee starting to work its magic, and the smooth jazz in the background coming from the speakers was also quite relaxing.

Annie looked at her hands, black from all the dust in her store. As she lowered her hands from her vision, she caught something in the corner of her eye. Turning back towards Herman's Curiosities, she saw a figure walking in front of the counter, and it looked like it was carrying a lit candle. Annie froze once again. Was someone in her store? Was she being robbed? Or was it something else? She decided to down her coffee, and head back, but as she left the coffee house, the light and the figure were gone.

"Dad, I'm telling you, someone was in the store."

Annie was trying hard not to shout down the phone, but her emotions were getting the best of her.

"I saw them, they had a candle and everything!"

"Angel, people don't rob stores at candle point. This is twenty-eighteen, if they use anything, it's probably laser drones or something."

"I know what I saw Dad, it was definitely a person." "Did you call the police?" Arthur asked.

"Well, no, I didn't."

Annie was trying hard to think why she hadn't done exactly that if she was so sure.

"And are you back in the store now, having this conversation?"

"Well, yeah."

"Then even you don't think there's a person in there. See? Psychology."

Annie hung up the phone and put it back on the counter. She had indeed walked right back into the store and sat back down. She had no fear there was a real person in there. And that's what really scared her. The fact that she was thinking paranormal more than criminal. Thoughts that were soon again at the front of her mind, when she heard a child's voice come from the front of the store.

She looked up but saw nothing. Then she heard it again. It sounded like screaming of some sort. The noise chilled her to the bone. Moving towards the source of the noise, she heard it again, this time louder, and this time it sounded like multiple people, not just one. The nearer she got to the front door, the louder the sounds became.

"*No, please not my little girl!*" "*Mommy? It hurts! It hurts so bad!*"

Then the talking stopped. Annie looked around but saw absolutely nothing. Then she felt a chill down her back as a cold air tickled her neck. She couldn't move, and as the feeling of someone standing right behind her became more intense, a tear formed in her eye. She stood her ground, closed her eyes, forced herself to spin around, and opened her eyes.

Nothing.

She glanced at the clock. Ten-twenty. Very late for a seventeen- year-old to be out alone in a creepy bookstore. Annie decided enough was enough, and she was done for the night. She moved towards the counter, all the time feeling like she was being watched, but when she got to the counter, her keys had gone.

A loud bang came from the back room. She jumped.

"Nope. Double nope. I am not going back there. Don't do it Annie, you don't wanna know what's in there."

As she warned herself not to go into the room, she was moving towards it, nonetheless.

"Why in the hell am I doing this?"

Another loud bang stopped her in her tracks. That didn't sound like an object falling, it sounded like a gunshot. Cautiously edging round the corner, Annie could smell smoke. Something hot or burning. Perhaps the aftermath of a gun firing, but she saw nothing to begin with. As she moved further into the room, very conscious of her own breathing, she could make out something on the carpet. She flicked the light switch, but no light came forwards, and as she glanced up, she could make out there was no actual bulb in the fitting.

She moved closer to the outline of the mass on the carpet. It looked like a damp patch. Curiosity now getting the better of her, she knelt over and placed a hand on it. Immediately she was hit with an icy cold feeling, and as she turned her hand over, she could see that this wasn't water on the floor. This was sticky and thick. Standing and moving back towards the light from the hallway, she raised her hand upwards, and her fears were confirmed. Blood trickled down her fingers.

Screaming, she turned and ran along the short hallway back into the main body of the store and was stopped in her steps by the sight of a man hanging from the ceiling fan.

Annie's heart was now racing faster than she could ever have thought possible, she looked down at her hands, and the blood was now gone, and when she looked back up, so was the hanging man.

"I need to get the hell out of here!"

Searching frantically for her keys, deliberately avoiding looking up in case more macabre spectacles awaited her, she kept her eyes to the ground and the surfaces of the benches and units. As she moved to the floor behind the counter, she stopped when she came face to face with a pair of shiny black shoes with wingtips, glimmering in the moonlight.

Slowly, she moved her gaze up the man's legs, and as she rose to her feet, she was face to face with what appeared to be a gangster styled gentleman, staring right through her. But what really caught her attention was the fact that her keys were in his hand.

"Looking for this sweetheart?"

The man's voice was cold and distant, and he didn't appear to be looking directly at Annie, but *through* her. She turned to see what he was looking at, but there was nothing there. She turned back and he was still standing there, hand outstretched, keys in the palm.

"W-w-w-what do you want from me?" she asked in her best brave voice.

He just looked through her, closed his hand and slid the keys into his pocket. A wry smile spread across his face. A look of pure evil. He slipped his hand inside his pinstripe jacket and pulled out a gun.

Annie's heart nearly burst from her chest, but she couldn't move. The man slowly raised his gun, and Annie tried everything she could to get herself to move, but it just wouldn't happen. Then she heard the bell crashing to the floor. She darted her head to the right to see Herman Fredericks backing away from the bell as it moved towards him. Her senses were overwhelmed right now.

She turned back towards the gangster who now had a terrified look on his face and was holding his hands above his head.

"No, please. Come on Frank, I was just kidding. I'd never do that to you. Please don't do it."

Annie spun around once more, and stood behind her was another man, heavy-set, also in a sharp suit, holding another gun, pointed in her direction.

"You're too late Donny. You crossed me one too many times. It's the end of the road for you."

He cocked his gun, and as he pulled the trigger, Annie dove to the floor, the sound of the bullet hitting Donny never came, just the sound of 7 gunshots. She scrambled along the floor, not daring to look back and as she finally got back to her feet, she came face to face with someone she had not expected to see.

Standing in the entrance to the store… was her mother. "Mom?"

Annie did not get a response. Her mother, Elizabeth, wasn't looking at her. Her form was almost transparent, and she was wearing the dress she'd had on the day she died. Annie had always focussed on the good memories of her mother and had blocked out the painful sight of her death. She had been hit by a car when Annie had just turned five. It wasn't until now, that she realised. Her mother had died outside this store.

She had been taking Annie to get a new book, and a drunk driver had mounted the curb. Elizabeth had pushed Annie out of the way and into the store, and the car had hit her instead.

"Mom, can you hear me?" asked Annie again, tears now streaming down her face.

Her mother turned around to walk out of the door but passed through it like it wasn't there. There was the sound of tyres screeching, a child screaming, and the shape of Elizabeth jerked to one side, rolled through the air and landed on the ground, where she faded away. Annie raised her hands to her mouth at reliving the horror of her mother's death. And then a light bulb moment.

She wasn't being haunted by ghosts or spirits as she knew them. She was being haunted by echoes of the past. Death that had occurred in and around this store throughout history were playing out. Residual energy, not intelligent spirits. She had such a strong connection to this building that she must be attracting them.

She turned back towards the counter to get her phone, which was now lit up with a phone call. She could see on the screen, 'Dad calling' but she didn't get to the counter. A faint call of a woman's voice stopped her dead.

"*Oh God no, Jesus protect me, please no!*"

The voice was coming from behind her. She slowly turned to face whatever sight would confront her, fists clenched tight, skin bright white. She saw a cloaked woman standing in front of the doorway once again. But this time, the woman she saw was not her mother, but an elderly woman. She let out a blood curdling scream, and held her hands up to her face, and she watched in horror as a man ran *through* Annie's body and swung an axe directly through the woman's throat. The man smiled with glee as the head of the elderly woman hit the floor. A huge cold blast of air hit Annie full on like a freight train, knocking her to the floor.

Her heart burst with such pain, she thought she was having a heart attack. Her eyes closed tight as she hit her head on the floor. Noises swirled around her, she covered her ears, and then all of it just stopped. She let go of her ears, and could hear carts in the distance, and the faint sound of *'Get your fresh fruits and vegetables, right from the farm.'*

When she opened her eyes, she was lying on the ground, outside, sunshine directly in her eyes. She placed her hands on the ground, but it wasn't the concrete she was used to, her hands were on cobbled stone. Still disorientated, she tried to get to her feet, but immediately staggered backwards. She felt a pair of strong hands grab her under the arms and catch her from falling back down. As she managed to compose her vision, she turned to look at the person who had caught her and was more than a little surprised.

"Not bad reflexes for an old man, Miss Annie."

"Mr Fredericks?"

Annie was certain she was hallucinating. She spun her head around three-sixty and what she saw confused her to her very core. A man was selling produce from a cart across the road, which was cobbled. There was a bank to her left, ornate, with iron bars on the windows, and well-dressed gentlemen walking in and out. The woman walking down the street wore long flowing dresses, and some of them began to stare back at her as they noticed her.

"It'll take a moment to get your bearings, try not to get too overwhelmed."

"But... where, am I? What happened? Where is the store? The ghosts?"

"Miss Annie, I promise you I will answer all your questions, but we should probably get you out of those clothes and into something more fitting for this time. It isn't so bad when you're an old man who appears in the street, but a young lady wearing a digital watch could cause quite a stir. After all, electricity hasn't been invented yet."

"What are you saying?"

Annie's face was full of panic, but also intrigue. She strangely felt at home.

"I'm saying… welcome to Victorian England, Miss Annie. You fell through the cracks."

"The ghosts at your store! They weren't ghosts, were they?"

Excitement now began to take over.

"I was right! They're residual energy from the traumatic events throughout history!"

Herman nodded.

"That's very true. Thought I'd died and gone to a strange variety of heaven, but I woke up just like you, in the street. Been here nearly eight years now. Got myself a little bookstore down the street there. Of course, all the books are brand new."

He winked at Annie. There was a shriek of a horse behind them, and a loud crash as a cart hit the side of the bank. Dozens of people rushed over to help, but the scene didn't look good.

Debris from the cart rolled into the street, and as Annie moved to follow Herman away from the scene, something struck her foot. Herman turned towards her.

"Stop kicking that bell Annie, and just pick it up."

SERPENTS & SKELETONS

I'd be very interested in seeing the results of your expedition, as due to the nature of my work, I am eager to obtain artefacts surrounding death for my new exhibition, which is due to open in October. If you do indeed uncover pieces of wreckage or perhaps jewellery from the wreckage, I would be willing to offer a fair price to expand my Deadly Possessions collection.

— *KIND REGARDS, KATHRYN SILVERTON.*

Steve read the email aloud to his fellow adventurers, or at least that's what they called themselves. He had of course spent the previous three years working as a janitor in a decrepit old mansion. The plan had gone without a hitch. Step one was to choose a suitable myth to investigate. Step two was to garner interest in making money from potential buyers of loot. Step three was finding something to sell. And finally, step four?

Well, that would be retiring to a private island filled with cash and naked women. At least that was the typically outdated dream of this group.

"Sounds pretty solid to me", said Alex. "After all, I'm hardly making any money from this stupid advertising gig. Whole thing's gone down the crapper since the boss took the eternal plunge off the Golden Gate bridge."

"Yeah, I mean there's worse things to be doing," agreed Frank.

He'd been out of work since the whole ghost hunting thing had fallen through.

"Besides, if this chick wants to buy creepy shit for her museum, then she's probably willing to pay top dollar."

Steve thought about it for a few minutes, and then shook his head.

"This must be genuine, and it has to be big. No fake reproductions, no plastic knock offs. If we're going after the *Sapphire Serpent*, then we must do it properly. We need the kit, we need the manpower, and we're gonna need the cash to get there."

"Who's going to be dumb enough to fork out thousands of dollars on hunting a myth?" asked Alex.

"I'll make some calls and see what I can drum up. See if there's anyone around this Kathryn chick who'd be willing to weigh in. Sounds like a growth industry, this ghost stuff."

The three men nodded in agreement, and each swivelled around in their chairs and began furiously typing into search engines and sending emails. Nobody used telephones these days, and within a few hours, each laptop had messenger notifications pinging from all directions.

"Okay, I got a guy in Idaho, who is willing to sponsor us five grand if we promise to give him sixty percent of what we find," said Frank. "But to be honest, he seems like kind of a whacko. His profile picture shows him clearly living in a basement with a poster of Marilyn Manson on the wall."

"No way are we getting involved with basement dwellers," replied Alex. "We're looking for ghost enthusiasts, not satanic worshippers."

"I think I may have got something."

Steve gestured to the others to move to his screen, and together they read the email he had received.

"That sounds promising. You don't get much closer than her personal financial advisor."

Alex read the email again, and just as he was finished, his own laptop pinged. As he slid across to read it, his face lit up.

"Hey, I've got another offer here, from some guy, Arthur, who says he'll be willing to put up fifteen grand."

"What is he asking in return?" asked Steve.

"He doesn't want anything. He just wants to be part of the journey, to seek answers to what happened to the ship. He's apparently just sold some store and is desperate to learn more about the afterlife. Sounds a bit loopy to me, but he is loaded."

Steve read the email, and after reading the full dialogue, his heart twinged a little with sadness. The man had clearly lost a lot, and given the circumstances, he could understand why he wanted to come.

"Okay, so we're agreed. We accept the two offers from this Arthur guy, and the financial advisor?"

The others nodded in agreement. "Then we have ourselves a trip."

"Couldn't you guys have rented a better van with the money I gave you?"

Kristin was not the camper van kind of girl. She was hunched up on what passed for a couch style seat next to Steve and a huge box of equipment.

"Hey, I thought you'd want your investment spent more wisely," replied Steve. "Besides, if we hit pay-dirt with this trek, you'll make a fortune."

"I'd better. I don't think Kathryn likes that I'm doing this. If I'm honest I think she's having second thoughts about opening the museum."

"I hope not. She's our biggest hope for a nice pay check."

"Some of us have more on our minds than money gentlemen."

Arthur spoke from the passenger seat but didn't turn around. He was too busy looking at the picture in his hand.

"Annie loved reading about pirates. Maybe she'll be good luck."

An awkward silence filled the van, until Alex broke it by announcing their arrival.

"Okay people, let's unload."

The dock was beautiful. The sun shone high above the water,

shimmering between the gentle waves. The water was a deep turquoise beyond the jetty, but beneath it, was crystal clear. A family of crab frittered underneath the boards, heading for shelter from the people now pounding their way towards their boat.

"That's it?"

Kristin's unimpressed questioning came as no surprise to the rest of the team. She'd complained she'd had to fly economy, then moaned about the quality of the food at the truck stop they'd eaten lunch at, and of course the van, so it made sense the 'ship' Alex had referred to would in fact be more like a dingy.

"All I ask is a tall ship, and a star to sail her by." Frank gazed at the modest vessel with admiration.

"Oh, please Frank, it's too early in the day for this *Star Trek* crap."

Steve moved past Frank, with a large case and stepped onto the aptly named 'Caribbean Sunset'.

Arthur followed carrying digging equipment, and Kristin, with her own significant suitcase. Alex locked up the van and tossed the keys to the nearby valet before joining the rest of the crew on board.

"Okay team, we all know why we are here, but let's set the scene."

Steve stood near the wheel, and the others sat below in front of him looking up like small children awaiting their bedtime story.

"We are here in the gorgeous port of Nassau for one reason. To find the wreckage of the Sapphire Serpent, the most notorious pirate vessel to never unload its treasure.

Captain Peter Easton, one of the most famous English born pirate Captains had just captured the Spanish ship '*San Sebastian*'. His acquisitions were quite sizeable, but the untold facts that became the legend we know of today, was that after capturing the San Sebastian, he came across a derelict pirate ship presumed to have been sunk by the British Navy. That ship was the *Sapphire Serpent*.

The holds were said to be bursting with treasure from all over the globe, but there was not a soul on board. Fearing that his enemies were growing, he is said to have taken control of the *Serpent* and entrusted one of his closest aides to sail her towards Nassau, far from the province of Newfoundland, and far from his enemies reach.

However, Easton never heard from the man again, and it was

assumed he'd taken the ship and the loot and started his own fleet. However, there are documented storms at that time, and records of the damage still exist to this day stating that over seventy-five ships were lost off the coast of Nassau, and historians believe it is highly likely that the *Serpent* was amongst them.

In the hundreds of years since these events, researchers have tracked and traced down every piece of factual evidence they can and have seemingly pinpointed the location of the wreck to somewhere within a thirty square mile radius of Thunderball Grotto. But even though it's near to highly populated areas, nobody has ever found it. Until now."

Alex and Frank had excited grins on their faces, but Kristin had another thought.

"What exactly is the evidence here?"

Steve looked disheartened that his storytelling prowess had not filled his guest with adventure.

"Celebrated explorers have discovered pirate coins on the seabed, and a chalice was discovered in a small rocky outcrop three miles from the shore. They have been dated in the early eighteen-hundreds."

"Oh yeah, I'm totally getting the Jack Sparrow vibes. Potential treasure without hard evidence. Next, you're gonna tell me you're bringing a jar of dirt for protection."

Despite her sarcasm, Kristin did begin to smile, which was reciprocated by Steve.

"Maybe we can stick together, I won't let the evil spirits get their hands on you," he suggested, stooping down in front of her.

"Yeah, then I can tell my girlfriend that all guys are indeed creeps, and she was right."

Kristin smiled through the words, speaking them just inches from his lips. A chorus of giggles and snorting came from behind her as Alex and Frank failed to contain their glee at watching their glorious leader being taken down a peg or two.

"Alright you clowns, let's get going. I want to make the first cave system by late afternoon."

Arthur took the wheel, and set the navigation for Thunderball Grotto, Frank released the rope from the dock, and Steve wound up the anchor, and as the sun shone down upon them, they made their way out into the bay.

As the Caribbean Sunset moved beyond the outcrop and entered the horizon, another vessel left the port in pursuit. The race for the treasure, it seemed, was on.

"Look I'm sorry, I didn't know you were in there!"

Alex took another battering from Kristin's wet towel, which now had left several thick red marks on his arm.

"How did you not hear the water running you moron!" she replied, still brandishing the towel.

"We're on water! It all sounds the same!"

Alex was now attempting to retreat to the top deck, if only to save himself from being whipped to death. Hearing the commotion, Arthur leaned over the rail into the cabin below to see what all the fuss was about.

"Can I lend any assistance Miss Kristin?" he asked politely.

"No thanks Arthur, just tell this pervert to check before walking in on a girl he doesn't know in the shower!" came the harsh reply.

Frank found the whole experience very entertaining.

"Dude, did you see anything?" he asked, despite Arthur's clear objections and looks of 'really?'

Alex simply made a 'wow' gesture, which earned him another whack with the towel. Steve interjected.

"Kristin, maybe you should put your hair towel away, and swap your body towel for some clothes. We're here."

The location was far from idyllic conditions for an amateur crew of explorers, and much departed from the paradise-like setting of Nassau and Thunderball Grotto. Since they headed out from the mainland, the conditions at sea had worsened and the rocky island they now found themselves at looked like a sore on the skin of the ocean.

Jagged formations jutted from the water, and nearby the remaining sections of wreckage from a more modern ship were visible, the wheelhouse mostly submerged, but the wheel itself shimmering in the low-hanging sun. No entrance was visible from the outside, however digital mapping showed an underwater entrance, and an opening about sixteen metres below the water's surface. The water itself was much more clouded than that of Nassau.

"Reminds me of Newquay," offered Arthur.

"Where?" asked Kristin.

Arthur smiled.

"A lovely little town on the Cornish coast in the UK. I used to take my daughter there for holidays. She'd always bring one of her books, but I'd always watch the waves for hours. Now that is a place with ghosts, my dear."

Intrigued, Kristin pressed for more details, but Arthur waved his hands away.

"I'll tell you more later, but you know the story of *the Woman in Black*? Well Newquay has the Girl in White."

"I hate to break up the spooky campfire stories here but prep yourselves for diving. It's a challenging route by the looks of it, and there's a tropical storm heading this way within the next eight hours. I'd like to be back towards the mainland by then."

Steve was already suited and booted, and ready to dive. Kristin, matching her 'out of my comfort zone' behaviour, had chosen a lilac wetsuit which she said was 'cute', but Arthur pointed out 'didn't leave much to the imagination'.

They leapt from the *Sunset* in sequence. Alex first, followed by Steve, then Arthur. Kristin wanted to go last on the suggestion that if she didn't Frank would be watching her ass instead of where he was going. He dived into the water, now very clouded from the multiple impacts, and as Kristin went to jump in, she could have sworn she saw moving figures on the edge of a rock jutting out into the sea. Just for a moment, she thought she caught the glow of a pair of eyes but dismissed it as the sun reflecting from the minerals.

As she leapt into the sea, she was indeed being watched, but it was by more than one pair of eyes.

"This is amazing," Arthur spoke, and his voice reverberated around the vast chamber they had emerged in. "It's like an ocean *TARDIS*."

"So, I can't make *Star Trek* references, but the old guy can quote *Doctor Who*?" Frank asked Steve in slight annoyance.

"Can we please focus?"

Steve was already unpacking lighting equipment, and Alex was helping him set it up.

"We need to start searching the cavern systematically and leave no rock unexplored. We have that deadline for the storm, and while we will be fine in here, I'd like to have a boat to go back to when we're done."

Kristin and Arthur switched on the lighting rigs and the cavern illuminated, the glare shimmering off the wet rocks. Each side to the chamber had its own unique shape, and there were pieces of wood almost consumed by the rock, their grains exposed only by the difference in shade to the rock itself. Drops of water echoed around them all, and lichen grew along the edges of the ledge they had emerged onto.

The entrance tunnel had opened central to the space they found themselves in, with other chambers of water, some smaller, some larger, dotted around the cave, like a network of veins connecting different parts of the island formation.

"Okay people, we know why we are here, so let's split into two teams. Alex, you go with Frank. Kristin and Arthur, you're with me. Guys you start with the left-hand side, we will start with the chambers on the right. Meet back in the centre here in two hours."

The teams went their separate ways, submerging themselves into the various pools on either side of the cave. Steve, Kristin and Arthur emerged into a smaller cavern, around four times smaller than the main chamber, and set up the secondary lighting rigs.

"That looks like a tunnel over there," Kristin pointed out.

It was indeed a tunnel, which appeared to snake around to the right, beyond which a faint shimmering light could be seen.

"I think you're right Kristin, that should be our first port of call."

Steve had become much more serious since they arrived, like he was firmly eyes on the prize. Arthur was still in a daze at the beauty of the place. He wondered what Annie would have made of all this. Her father was never one for adventures, but he had found a newfound interest since he'd lost her.

As the trio made their way towards the tunnel entrance, they heard a cracking sound that stopped them in their tracks.

"Did you hear that?" asked Arthur.

"Yeah, and it didn't sound good," replied Kristin. "It could be seismic."

"I don't think so," replied Steve. "That sounded more like something snapping."

The trio looked around but couldn't see any movement, so they dismissed it and continued towards the tunnel entrance. However, when they reached it, there was a bang that echoed around the entire cave system and all the lights went dead.

"Fucking marvellous."

Kristin cautiously sat down in the darkness, not willing to try and navigate jagged rocks in the dark.

"Calm down moneybags, it's probably just a fuse. Electrics and water tend not to mix."

Steve pulled out an emergency torch from his backpack and clicked it into life. It wasn't very powerful, but it was enough to see what was in front of him. Or at least, what should have been in front of him. The lighting rigs were gone. The only evidence that they had been there, were slight tracks in the sand lying on top of the rocky ledge.

"Where the fuck are my lights?"

Steve was now becoming unsettled. This fear only escalated when through the darkness, they heard the water rippling, and the faint sound of a hiss.

"What was that?" Kristin asked, now with a much more high-pitched voice than her original outburst. "Arthur, can you see anything?"

Silence.

"Arthur?" Kristin asked again.

Steve turned to shine his flashlight on Kristin, but the beam could not locate Arthur.

"Arthur?"

Steve's voice joined the search for their companion but couldn't find him. They were disturbed again, when the hissing became much louder, and the sound of bubbling water could now be heard.

"Steve, where's Arthur? And what the hell is that?"

"I don't know, but I don't like the sound of it. Arthur? Where are you buddy?"

Kristin backed up into the tunnel, on all fours to avoid the pointed walls, while Steve frantically shone his flashlight around the chamber. Suddenly, his beam caught the outline of a figure. He focused the light on it and squinted his eyes. Kneeling over the edge of the ledge looking deep into the water, was Arthur.

"Arthur, buddy, what are you doing?"

Arthur didn't respond. His gaze was captured by something in the water. Something Steve couldn't see. Steve gradually began to move towards Arthur, feeling his way along the rock face.

"Come on Arthur, come away from there."

Steve closed to within six feet of Arthur, when the cave filled with the sound of hissing and disembodied moans, and before his very eyes, a hand reached out of the water, grabbed onto Arthur's head and pulled him into the pool, leaving not even a splash behind him.

Steve screamed and lunged backwards, hitting his head on a jagged piece of stone, and falling to the floor, sending his torch scattering across the floor into the pool in which Arthur had just disappeared. Kristin scrambled her way across the floor feeling for Steve.

"Steve! Oh my god, what the hell is happening? Steve! Can you hear me?"

Steve groaned, blood trickling down the back of his head. Kristin reached him, trying to feel for his face in the dark.

"Steve, come on, I need you to tell me what happened!"

"Something took Arthur, Kristin, it took him."

"What do you mean something took him?"

"It reached up out of the water and took him!"

The moaning started again, and they could hear footsteps landing on wet rock. The squelching and moaning became more intense. The only light was now the dull shimmering light coming from the end of the tunnel.

"Come on Steve, we need to get down this tunnel."

Kristin tried to drag Steve closer to the light, and he managed to turn and began moving on his hands and knees behind her. The footsteps became louder and more pronounced, almost as if someone was now hunting them down. Kristin kept looking towards the light, edging closer and closer, Steve barely keeping up with her. She could now see the blood dripping down the side of his face in what little light there was.

As they managed to manoeuvre around the corner, a piercing scream echoed from beneath them, and the sound of two loud bangs in quick succession. The footsteps retreated and Kristin and Steve stopped their movements.

"Did that sound like Alex?" asked Steve.

"Yeah, and gunshots."

Kristin was trembling, and as she looked down, noticed she too had caught the rocks, and had a three-inch gash in the side of her thigh. They both listened for a minute but heard nothing.

"We need to keep moving. I don't know what is happening here, but I know I don't wanna stick around to find out."

Steve started crawling again, and Kristin followed.

They finally emerged into another chamber, but what was casting the light took their breath away. Laying at an impossible angle, embedded through the cave wall, was the bow of the *Sapphire Serpent*, an opening in the roof allowing the now rising moon to shine through. Below the water in front of them, catching that moonlight, was hundreds of thousands of gold coins.

"No, please, don't."

Frank's face was streaming with tears, blood splattered across his face, his eyes unable to move from the lifeless body of Alex, his eyes wide open, blood pouring from the hole in his head, and his clothes soaked with the blood from the hole in his chest. The figure moved towards him, gun to their side.

"What do you want? We haven't found anything!"
"No, and that is how I'd like it to stay."

Bewitched by what they were seeing, Steve and Kristin attempted to take it all in. Realising she was still bleeding quite badly, Kristin tore the sleeves off her wetsuit, tied one around her leg, and the other around Steve's head to apply pressure.

Two more gunshots rang out.

"Shit, Steve, we need to get the hell out of here!"

Kristin scanned for a way up to the opening in the rock.

"We found it."

Steve's eyes were fixed on the gold.

"Steve, we need to go now!"

"I can't believe we found it. It's so beautiful."

"Steve?"

"So beautiful."

Steve began moving into the water.

"Steve, what are you doing? We need to leave! Something is coming!"

Steve continued his descent into the water, hands reached out in front of him, grasping towards the gold medallions. Kristin jumped down from the ledge she had stepped onto, and ran towards him, but stopped just short of the waterline, when she saw what was making its way through the water.

Emerging from all sides, were dark figures, bones exposed to the moonlight, rags for clothes, hands outstretched, moving below the water towards Steve. The moans began again, and hissing began to come from the bow of the ship.

"STEVE!"

Kristin shouted the best she could, but it was no use. As the figures dragged Steve below the water's surface, he turned his head and spoke in a trance.

"So beautiful."

Kristin stared in horror as Steve vanished into the abyss, and his body sank into the piles of gold.

A massive explosion rocked the cavern, sending chunks of rock cascading from the sky into the water, and striking the bow of the *Serpent*, carving a huge chunk out of the green snake figurehead. Kristin barely managed to keep her balance. She didn't have time to waste, and wiping the tears away from her face, she turned to head back towards the opening in the roof.

"That's quite far enough I'm afraid."

Standing in front of Kristin, pointing a gun directly at her head, was a Mexican man, who she faintly recognised.

"I've been on one too many expeditions to let a haul like this pass me by."

"Do I know you?" Kristin asked.

She was almost certain she knew the face from somewhere but couldn't place it. She was also acutely aware of the danger she was currently in from whatever was lying beneath the water next to her.

"Ah, how rude of me not to introduce myself. My name is Carlos Rodriguez. And I'm taking this treasure, if you don't mind."

Then the image clicked. Kristin had seen Rodriguez on the news following an expedition to Antarctica.

"Did you kill your partner too?" she asked him. Carlos chuckled.

"Actually, no. Jonathan was somewhat accident prone. He was never careful enough with where he stuck his cock or his feet. But I've had enough of not coming home with anything but disappointment and an empty bank balance. Everyone wanted to finance Jonathan's trips, but never mine. This time, I'm taking all the glory, and the treasure."

He raised the gun again, and Kristin's eyes were drawn to the water, which had begun moving again. She slowly started to move around, steps which Carlos matched. She decided to keep him talking.

"Doesn't it bother you that this treasure was so easy to find? And yet nobody has ever found it? Something is living in this island, in this water. And it doesn't want this treasure taken."

Kristin stopped when Carlos had his back facing the *Serpent*. The dark figures in the water moved closer.

"The only things living on this island at the moment are you and I madam. A problem I intend to eradicate momentarily."

The figures of skeletal demons emerged from the water and just as they reached Carlos, his expression changed, as he felt their presence behind him. Kristin's face became resolute, and she stared him directly in the eyes.

"You might wanna check that with them."

Dozens of decaying hissing pirate corpses piled onto Carlos from behind, hands grasping at his face, tearing his wetsuit, blood visible on his face, and chest. He tried to struggle free, but the crew of the *Sapphire Serpent* were too strong.

Shrieking echoed around the caverns, and tunnels. Carlos' gun fired, just missing Kristin, as she kept herself pressed against the wall, the rocks digging into her back. Carlos thrashed in the water, sending splashes of ocean and blood, and coins scattering through the air. His cries were almost deafening.

A few of the coins and medallions landed at Kristin's feet. As Carlos finally vanished below, she lunged forward, grabbed two medallions, and scrambled up the rock face as quickly as she could. The cries gradually faded away, and as Kristin emerged on top of the island, there was one final shriek, and then silence.

As she stumbled down the side of the island formation, she saw the *Caribbean Sunset*. Or at least, what remained of it. The hull was gone, sunk below the waterline, with just a few pieces of burning wreckage left floating on the surface. Carlos had clearly not intended to them to escape. Another few moments of scanning the ocean, and she spotted a smaller craft, anchored off the far edge of the island.

She cautiously moved down the side of the rocks, the wind now getting very powerful, and the clouds beginning to move across the sky. She reached the sea, and prepared herself to leap into the dark waters, knowing what she had faced inside.

Taking a deep breath, she leapt into the abyss, narrowly missing several outcrops below the surface. As she kicked her way back towards the surface, she turned and saw the faces of the men that had accompanied her here. Hanging motionless in the depths were the empty eyes of Steve, Alex, Frank and Arthur. And lower down, was the figure of Carlos, held down by undead hands. Kristin turned away and kicked her way back into the night air, and swam her hardest to Carlos' boat, not looking back again.

"So, are you going to tell me how you got this or what?"

Kathryn was trying her best to get some form of explanation. The piece was exquisite and was clearly hundreds of years old.

"I'm telling you, it came from the *Sapphire Serpent*, guaranteed and that's all you need to know."

Kristin had not gone into the details since she got back.

"So, what happened, did you kill the nerds you bankrolled," Kathryn joked.

Kristin smiled falsely.

"Look sweetie, you wanted deadly possessions, and I can tell you, I've never seen an object more shrouded in death than that medallion."

Kathryn looked slightly concerned and placed a hand on the side of Kristin's face. Kristin closed her eyes in appreciation of the comfort.

"Okay, let's go put it in its new case. I can finally finish my pirate exhibit."

Kathryn walked past the John Martin room and into the pirate room. She opened a glass case, and slipped the medallion inside, closing the case afterwards.

"Looks good," Kristin offered.

"Yeah, I think I'm happy with that. Think I might turn this room into a whole pirate treasure, ghost, kinda exhibition."

"Sounds great, the people will love it. How are you doing after your whole ordeal?"

"I'm okay. Funny thing is, this is where I feel safest now. Feels like a lot of people have my back."

Kristin smiled.

"So, you wanna go get a coffee? There's still a lot of planning to do before you do your Halloween Event, and only two days left."

"Are you buying? Or do financial advisors not put their hand in their own pocket?"

Kathryn grinned, and Kristin responded.

"I do actually have money, you know."

"Prove it."

Kristin plunged her hand into her bag, pushed the second medallion to one side, and pulled out her purse.

"See?"

"Alright, but I want a large one."

"Yeah, you always did until I came along."

Kathryn opened her mouth in shock at the speed of the comeback and gave Kristin a cheeky slap on the arm.

"Okay, let's go. Oh, and remind me, I think those new Stevenson dolls would be more at home in the attic with the others."

RED CHRISTMAS

The fanfare truly was something out of a holiday movie. It was beyond what one would describe as 'over the top' and was still building. The stage in front of the store was surrounded by thousands upon thousands of multi-coloured fairy lights, flashing in waves, whilst around the main stage floor, confetti cannons would periodically fire into the crowd. The DJ was blasting out head banging tunes at a volume intended to reach God, and the sheer volume of fast-food stands was enough to rival a hundred carnivals. As the music began to die down, the mayor approached a microphone, which was itself covered in red, white and blue tinsel and flanked by two seven-foot Christmas trees.

"Ladies and gentlemen, thank you for attending the opening of the greatest store this country has ever known!"

The crowd erupted in cheers and whooping and screaming as if they were present at a rock concert for a legendary performer. Buoyed up by the crowd, and unused to this kind of attention, particularly so positive, the mayor continued.

"I just want to thank the planning committee for seeing the potential behind this move, and of course the CEO of M.V. Stores, Mr. Steve Zane!"

Again, the crowd erupted into cheers as the business mogul appeared on stage to replace the mayor at the microphone. He was very much in the same mould as Jeff Bezos, Bill Gates, and Elon Musk. Great products, but questionable morals. He flashed a winning smile, almost as bright as the lights behind him, before gesturing to the crowd to quieten down and allow him to speak.

"Thank you, Mr. Mayor, and thanks to all of you for joining us at this opening ceremony. When I founded M.V. Stores back in 2010, I knew that we would just keep moving forward at a breakneck speed. Nobody would stop us from bringing quality products at affordable prices to every town in America, and we would have a store in every state within five years. And here we are, opening our one-hundred and twenty-fifth store right here in Trinity Bay!"

The fanfare continued, and again the crowd obeyed the signal to become quiet. Zane had them trained and trained well.

"As with all of our flagship stores, we have chosen to open during the holiday season, just in time for all of your Christmas shopping needs. As you know, M.V. Stores stands for Maximum Velocity. And that is exactly what we are doing here today. Incredible deals coming at you at top speed in the form of 30% off all final totals at the checkouts for the first hundred customers through the door!"

More cheers from the crowd, another silenced gesture.

"We have inside this store, and incredible array of items you cannot find anywhere else! You can even buy a top-of-the-line security system from our salespeople in store. How good you say? So good, that they are the very same systems we are using to protect the store itself. And right now, they're 20% off! So… let's get this show on the road!"

Zane held the ribbon taught, and as the crowd began to put real pressure on the barriers, the mayor cut the fabric, declaring the new store open, and as soon as the guards opened the barriers, a tidal wave of human vultures burst through, shoving others to the ground, and trampling on those unfortunate enough to end up on the ground. Zane and the Mayor disappeared out of sight as the crowd swelled over the stage, the Christmas trees falling victim to the surge.

For the rest of the day, the inside of the vast warehouse type store was pure carnage. Security was involved on dozens of occasions, breaking up violent altercations between parents vying for the last *Avengers* toys, or grandmas fighting it out over the last roll of candy pink wool for their knitted scarves.

By the time the announcement came that the store was closing for the night, over three quarters of the shelves were decimated. One by one the checkouts began to close, and security began waving people goodnight. It had been quite a day, and there was still Christmas Eve to go. As the staff began to steel themselves up for another assault the following day, not everyone was preparing to leave.

"Hey, Ben? You there?"

A head popped out from between two life sized teddy bears. "Yeah Nat, I'm over here!"

The two moved out into the back of the toy aisle, where they were joined by three others, all dressed in coats and black woolly hats. Checking around for the security cameras, and the store patrols, they discussed their plan.

"Okay, so we have fifteen minutes until the doors come down. I want us spread out across the toy section. Ben, you get back between the stuffed animals. Dean, you go for the Wendy house in the back yard display, and make sure you're covered up. Jodie, I want you in the space rocket in the Buzz Lightyear display, and Keenan, you can conceal yourself in the camping scene by the outdoor gear, so you have a clear view of the entrance. I'll slip between the shelving units on the back wall where the customers have dislodged the units. We all clear on the plan?"

Nodding heads moved around the circle, before they were disturbed by incoming footsteps.

"Okay, move!" Nat whispered, and she vanished, along with the four others.

One by one, the lights clicked out across the ceiling, the sound of powering down echoing around the vast space. In between the shelving units on the back wall, a very dim blue light was visible as Nat put her plan into action. A plan which was confirmed to have been successful when the security guards realised an issue with the new systems.

"Hey Steve, you seein' this?"

"What is it?"

"Cameras are off. All of 'em."

"Quality security systems my ass. Old man just couldn't be bothered to pay someone to install a proper system."

"So, what do I do? Call support?"

"Haha, you gotta be shittin' me. It's two days before Christmas. They're off in the Bahamas by now. Nah, just activate the shutters and the deadbolts, and leave the cameras and laser systems off for the night."

"Lasers too?"

"If we don't have cameras to verify the laser trips are being set off by rats or whatever, then we'll be up and down here all night. You want that?"

"Hell no."

"So shut it down, and let's get the hell out of here. The wife is cookin' brisket tonight."

A smile crept onto the slightly illuminated face of Natalie as she put her phone back into her pocket and kept still until the coast was clear. But they weren't intending to be too eager. Keenan watched on from his tent as the doors were locked and the armoured roller shutters slammed down to the ground. That was it. They were in for the night. He waited for another ten minutes, before giving the signal.

"Hooty-hoo!" he exclaimed in a high-pitched voice.

One by one, the team of five emerged from their hiding places. As Nat climbed out of the shelving, she looked up at the CCTV cameras, to see that indeed the system was off, and no visible light was on the cameras themselves.

"You're gonna have to show me how you did that sometime," Dean joked as he patted Nat on the back.

"That's the benefit of having a dad with a security company. Everyone else's systems are bullshit."

"So where do we start?" asked Jodie, still picking bits of cotton wool from her hair from the fake clouds in the display.

"Well, the money is gonna be locked down in the safe, and there's no way we can get through there inside of two hours. And it's too early to start drilling through the wall, we might arouse suspicion. So, for now, let's just find the tools we need, and get some food."

Keenan was slightly put off with such a relaxed approach, but he hadn't eaten since lunch so decided to just roll with it, and he and Ben headed for the food section, while Nat, Jodie and Dean headed for hardware.

First thing on their list was a diamond edge saw. Using a discarded shopping trolley, they whizzed around the aisles collecting the replacement blades, the sledgehammers, and anything else they thought they might need to break the safe open with. They even thought to grab spare phone chargers in case Nat's battery died and they lost their connection to the system. When the staff came back in the morning, they would switch it back on to see if it was still malfunctioning, and Nat needed to make sure it was.

Placing the tools at the far end of the line of cash registers, they joined up with the others who were using a hot plate to cook up pancakes in the camping display.

"Dude, what are you doing? You wanna set off the smoke detectors?" Nat exclaimed, switching off the power, and trying her best to wave the smoke away.

"Hey, I just thought we could have a nice campfire style hangout, you know, while we wait to become rich," Kenan replied.

A loud bang from the other side of the store broke up the argument, and all five members of the little gang snapped their heads in that direction.

"What in the hell was that?" asked Dean.

Nat held her hand up for quiet, and slowly stood up, gesturing for the others to do the same. She pulled out her phone, and checked the hack was still intact. It was. Although the cameras were off, the programme was still running just in case. She resisted the urge to turn them back on to investigate, for fear of them being discovered on one of the feeds. Another bang, this time followed by the sound of a trolley moving along the floor.

"Yo, this shit is not what I signed up for, Nat."

Keenan was beginning to freak out. Somebody was pushing a cart down one of the aisles, but all five of them were accounted for.

"Okay, we need to check it out."

"Are you crazy?" asked Jodie. "We need to hide out, in case we get spotted!"

Nat looked her square in the eyes.

"We got here first, and that money is ours. If somebody else is here, we need to deal with that. Now."

She nudged Dean and Ben, and the three of them headed toward the sound of the noise, which was still happening. Jodie and Keenan stayed back where they were. There was no way they were getting involved in a fight of any kind.

As Nat and the other two moved along the store, the sound of the trolley got louder. They couldn't tell if they were getting closer to it, or it was coming to meet them. Finally, Nat suggested they stop, but the second they did, so did the trolley.

"What the hell?" Dean mouthed to Ben.

Another bang. This time, loud enough and close enough to make all three of them leap in the air. It had come from the next aisle, but there was no wall in that aisle, just shelving. This was more like someone banging on a concrete wall. Nat cautiously led the other two around the corner of the aisle, where they found their trolley, filled with the power tools and accessories, pointing towards them. As the fourth bang echoed around the store, they watched the trolley physically move with the vibration. Whatever it was, it was directly below the trolley. *Under the floor.*

"What is that the basement?" asked Dean.

"Must be," Nat acknowledged. "Wonder how we get down there."

"Woah, why would we want to get down there?" asked a now more panicked Ben.

"We need to find out what the hell that is! That noise could blow our whole operation!" Nat fired back.

But there was one question still not being answered, and Dean wanted to bring it up.

"How come none of you are asking how that trolley got here in the first place?"

"Well, let's find our way to the basement and maybe we can find out."

Nat signalled them to split up and take three different directions towards the doors marked 'Staff Only' and they would meet there. Meanwhile Keenan and Jodie were still sat on camping stools next to the now cold hot plate.

"Look, I don't know what's going on here, but I just signed up to make some quick money and pay off my student loans. Ain't no way I am getting arrested or beaten up. This ain't what I agreed to."

Jodie agreed with Keenan, as she pulled off her sixth acrylic nail with the stress and dropped it to the floor.

"Maybe we should go and hide back in our original places, until this is all over and done with. I mean nobody knew we were there right, so they wouldn't know if we went back."

Keenan nodded, and they stood up, before Jodie stopped them to clarify a point.

"But we should pick one of our places and both hide out together. You know, for safety."

"Yeah. Yeah, for safety."

Holding hands, they edged their way away from the camping set up and headed slowly back towards the toy department. A scratchy object brushed Jodie's face, and she jumped back, and let out a scream, before falling on her backside. As Keenan shined his torch on the object, he let out a long-relieved sigh. It was just a branch of an artificial Christmas tree sticking out.

But the relief was short lived. From somewhere in the toy department, came the sound of mechanical laughter. Both Keenan and Jodie froze where they were.

"What the fuck was that?" whispered Keenan.

Jodie simply shook her head in terror and tried to get back to her feet. But as she put weight on her left foot, the small heel on her boot broke off, and she clattered to the floor once more. The laughter came again.

"Somebody is laughin' at us, man."

"I don't like this, Keenan. Something is wrong. Somebody is watching us!"

Keenan helped Jodie back to her feet, and against every fibre of their being, they once again began to slowly make their way towards the toys. Another object knocked to the floor by Jodie's long jacket made her jump, which in turn generated more laughter. Their blood was running cold, and their bodies were consumed by goosebumps, and they were still a clear two-hundred feet away from their proposed destination, such was the size of the building.

Suddenly, another noise came into range, and the pair stopped.

"What's that?" asked Jodie.

Keenan simply shrugged, and shone his torch in all directions, looking for the source. It was like the trolley noise, but it was coming from something smaller. Then the sound of a toy fire engine could be heard. The confusion and surprise on both faces was evident to each other, and finally, Keenan's torch came to rest on the toy itself, rolling towards them, slowly, lights flashing and siren whirring. As they watched, the little plastic ladder extended upwards, and Jodie could see something shiny was attached to the end but couldn't quite make it out. The truck stopped six feet away, and the pair just looked at it.

Keenan was now becoming irritated by how little control they seemed to have over the situation and felt the anger rising in his chest.

"What?! What you want?!"

With that display of anger, the fire truck came to life again, and barrelled towards him at speed, and as it crashed into his shin, Keenan jumped into the air with pain, collapsing onto the floor. More laughter from the toy department.

"What is it?" asked Jodie, now terrified.

"Fucking thing stabbed me!" cried Keenan.

And sure enough, as they looked down at Keenan's shin, the little plastic ladder was sticking out of his skin, now separate from the toy itself. As Keenan pulled it free, they saw attached to the end was a small Stanley knife replacement blade. Now they knew something was up.

Over the other side of the store, Nat had been trying not to get distracted by the extra noises happening all around her, and had her eyes fixed on the 'Staff Only' double doors. As she closed in, a white mist flew past the windows of the doors, on the other side. She stopped. A moment or two later, it went past again. Not a typical cartoon ghost shape, but a mass of some kind.

As she started moving towards it again, the doors moved. They swung gently on their hinges, and Nat's eyes lowered to the handles. The movement stopped. But as she looked back up at the windows, a face was looking back at her on the other side of the glass. She screamed, and stumbled backwards, and the face shot out of view. As she held her hand to her mouth and tried to regulate her breathing, she braced herself against the shelves next to her.

The face had not been that of a human. It was pale, misshapen and had black pits where the eyes should have been. It may have been the shock of it, but she also could have sworn it had horns atop of its head. After a moment or two, her rational mind kicked in again, and she suspected whoever else was in there with them, was wearing a disguise. Perhaps a Halloween mask of some sort. Either way she needed to know and began moving towards the doors once more.

Ben, meanwhile, was walking along the line of checkouts, trying to see if anyone was hiding between them, but had found nothing. He took a seat next to a row of child sized vending machines containing little toys in eggs, and bouncy balls.

Pulling a hip flask from his jacket, he took a swig of mulled wine. It was Christmas after all. As he replaced the flask in his pocket, a bouncy ball ejected itself from the machine next to him and bounced away out of sight. He turned to look at the mechanism. It seemed fine, but just to be sure gave it a little jiggle. Nothing came out, so he let go, and looked back off into the distance. Another ball came out and bounced along the floor. But this time, as he looked at the machine again, the dial began turning, and turned consistently without stopping, launching bouncy ball after bouncy ball out of the machine.

He stood up and slowly began to back away, always keeping his torch on the machine. Behind him, he thought he could feel someone watching him. He stopped and turned around and sat on the floor directly in front of him, was a teddy bear. The fact the bear was there didn't confuse Ben at all. What he was having trouble with, was understanding how the bear came to be wearing a pair of sunglasses and holding a hunting knife.

Ben began to back up towards the vending machines again, but as that kicked into overdrive and began shooting out the toys as well as the bouncy balls, he moved between the checkouts. The bear, however, turned its head to follow him.

"Uh, guys?" he called out into the darkness. "Guys, some weird shit is happening here. Anybody?"

No answer came, and Ben failed to pay attention to where he was walking. His left foot met a cluster of bouncy balls and he slipped backwards, reaching out for a surface to steady himself on, but missed the edge of the checkout.

As he fell backwards, his head hit the marble floor, and a sickening crack echoed around the checkouts. A wave of sickness came over him, and he began to lose consciousness. He reached a hand up to his head, and sure enough, found a small puddle of blood forming. He had also dropped his torch, and as he fumbled for it with what remained of his strength, his fingertips caught it. But as he raised it to shine the light in front of him, the beam met the face of the bear, and as Ben let out a muffled scream, the teddy bear plunged the knife down into his chest, cracking through a couple of ribs on the way to his heart.

As Ben choked on his own blood, the last whisper of life left his body, and the torch went dead.

Convinced he had heard somebody scream, Dean shone his own torch towards the front of the store, but after a moment, decided he had imagined it and turned back towards his destination, only to bump right into Nat. The two of them screamed and pushed away from each other, before realising who they had confronted, and slowly began to calm down.

"I thought you were heading for the back room?" he asked her.

"I was, but I saw somebody back there through the doors, and I came to find you guys. Where's Ben?"

"I don't know. He went to check out the front of the store. Probably still there. Wait, what do you mean you saw somebody?"

Nat described the face to him and the white mass, but his face was a picture of disbelief, so she grabbed his arm and dragged him back towards those very same doors. As they both cautiously peered through the windows, they saw nothing but packed shelving, and an open door to the left of the freezers.

"That must be it," Nat pointed out. "The door to the basement. If it's open, that must be where they went."

"Hey, wait a minute," Dean protested, but before he completed his sentence, Nat was through the doors, so he followed her.

She stopped next to a computer that she presumed was used to log deliveries and grabbed an object off the desk. Brandishing it as a weapon, she turned to Dean to get his opinion.

"A pricing gun? Really? What are you gonna do, reduce them to death? Special Christmas savings on psychopaths, now fifty percent off!"

Throwing the object on the ground, Nat responded aggressively.

"Okay genius, you find something!"

Dean looked around and spotted a high visibility coat, hard hat and truncheon hanging on a coat rack near the staff entrance.

"Must belong to one of the guards," he said as he walked over and picked it up.

Now feeling like they were finally armed, the two of them headed down into the basement, and as they did so, the door gently closed behind them, and the lock clicked into place.

The toy section may have been in another store entirely, it was taking Keenan and Jodie that long to get there. Every time they walked past another aisle, they heard movement, and felt somebody watching them. The laughter, at least, had ceased for now. But as they made their way through the sporting goods department, a familiar festive sound made their blood run cold.

From far behind them, came the sound of jingle bells. At first it could have been mistaken for distant Christmas music coming from somewhere outside, but the more intensely they stared into the darkness, the louder the bells became and not only that, but they seemed to be getting closer.

"This place is beyond fucked up," Keenan pointed out.

He was now so traumatised, and his leg was still causing him a mild pain, that his tolerance for this adventure was gone.

"Where is that coming from?" asked Jodie, still trying to be as ignorant as possible because she feared what the truth may be.

"*Ho...ho...ho...*"

The booming voice seemed to vibrate the floor tiles at their feet. The sound of jingle bells continued, and then fairy lights began to illuminate in their boxes along the shelving, coming on one box at a time, casting shadows across the floor. Again, the voice boomed.

"*Ho...ho...HO!*"

Completely frozen, Jodie and Keenan had their gaze fixed on what was coming out of those shadows, and the disbelief at what they were seeing almost blew their minds. As '*Jingle Bell Rock*' began playing out of the tannoy speakers, the giant inflatable Santa Claus that had been stood at the store entrance during the day, lumbered into view, eyes glowing red.

"*Someone has been naughty this Christmas!*"

Keenan looked right at the inflatable menace.

"Fuck this shit!"

He span on his heels and sprinted as fast as he could away from the horrific scene which resembled a horror comedy, leaving Jodie still stuck on the spot, unsure if this was real, or a nightmare. Her eyes were wider than seemed possible, and she was shivering in her coat. As Santa got closer, the painted expression on the fabric of his face, morphed into something far more sinister. The mouth widened and curled upwards, and the lips parted to reveal rows and rows of sharpened teeth.

"*Good boys and girls get candy canes, Jodie. Do you know what naughty boys and girls get?*"

Compelled to answer, Jodie shook her head. Santa smiled even wider.

"*Naughty boys and girls get punished!*"

The two arms of the polyester body flew out to the side and summoned some unseen power. The fairy lights erupted from their boxes and flew towards Jodie like possessed vines of ivy, wrapping themselves around her limbs and tightening their grip. As they glowed more intensely, the cord wrapped itself around Jodie's throat getting ever tighter. Each gasped breath seemed to make the lights brighter, as the demonic Santa watched on gleefully. Jodie's entire body was lifted from the floor, suspended by the lighting cables which had now wrapped themselves around one of the ceiling beams, and with one final thrust from Santa's arms, the cord penetrated the skin of her throat, and sliced her windpipe.

The music died out, and the inflatable monster collapsed back into a pile of nothing more than fabric. The jingle bells faded into the distance, and the only remaining sound was the dripping of Jodie's blood onto the hard floor below.

The basement was lit eerily by red emergency lights which lined the exposed pipework at the top of each wall. Clearly the building had been finished in a rush to get it open in time for the holidays, and there were still parts that were not complete. The basement was one of those parts. At the bottom of the stairwell, the tiles and the concrete had simply run out. Nat and Dean were now walking on exposed sand and gravel, struggling to see ahead of them.

"Why don't you just use your phone flashlight?" Dean pointed out.

"Look, if I drain the battery on my phone, and the system somehow comes back online, we lose our connectivity, and we're fucked. Use yours!"

Dean reached into his pocket and pulled out his phone. Holding it proudly before her face, he declared 'There weren't flashlights on phones in nineteen-ninety-seven."

Nat stepped back to focus on what was being thrust at her, and realised she was looking at the wonder of an original Nokia 3310. Despite the situation, she turned towards Dean and displayed a look of confusion. After everything she had seen so far tonight, and not been able to explain, this was by far the most perplexing.

"We live in the year twenty-twenty-three, and you have a Nokia 3310? You weren't even alive when that phone was out!"

Withdrawing his pride and joy, and displaying his own bemused look, Dean put the device away before responding.

"It was my mothers' phone."

Nat felt regret and shame immediately and placed a reassuring hand on his shoulder. Dean had lost his mother when he was very young, when a tornado hit their house. He'd never really known her, but his father had told him all about her as he grew up. She had been into some weird shit, though. The kind of stuff that they were involved in at that very moment. And thinking about that gave Nat an idea. An idea that was further thrust into her mind when her foot crunched over something.

"What was that? Glass?" Dean asked.

Against her better judgement, Nat got out her phone and switched on the light. She had not trodden on glass. She had trodden on *bones*. Rodent bones, to be specific. Clearly, they had a problem here. But the rat bones weren't the ones she was now staring at. Just beyond those, her light illuminated a red line, which followed around in a large circle in the dirt. The gravel and sand had been swept aside to provide clear definition. The lines jutting out from the circle crossed each other towards the centre, and then crossed out again to meet the far side of the circle. Within the confines of the image before them, were chicken bones, dark red stains which were visible even through the tint of the artificial red light and burned down candles.

"Is that what I think it is?" she asked Dean.

"It's a pentagram. A used one, at that."

Almost on cue, came a loud banging noise on the door at the top of the stairs. They turned to look in that direction, and whilst their attention was distracted, the white mist returned. It curled upwards from the circle and swirled into what appeared to be a humanoid shape, albeit with no discernible features.

Dark voids emerged where there should be eyes, and the mist at the top of the figure darkened and extended into a horn-like feature on either side of the head. Feeling like something was behind her, Nat slowly turned around and as she opened her mouth to scream, the entire entity shot forth and slid into her open mouth. The banging on the door above continued, and was keeping Dean's attention as the remaining mist vanished inside Nat.

When the audible sound of Keenan's voice became discernible amongst the banging, Dean shot back up the stairs where he saw his friends' terrified face.

"Hey man, the door's locked!" he bellowed.

Dean made his way towards the top of the stairs, but as he reached the fourth step down, two hands erupted from either side of his feet and gripped the bottom of his legs. The hands were ice cold, deathly white, with long yellow fingernails scratching at him. Dean fell forwards, and tried to hold onto the handrail for support, but it came away from the wall. As the holes surrounding his feet became larger, more hands came out from the disintegrating concrete, tugging at him until the entire staircase caved in, and Dean along with the dead clawing hands, vanished into the darkness. The only evidence that he had been there, was his mothers' Nokia 3310, which had bounced down the bottom couple of stairs, along the floor and came to rest in the centre of the pentagram.

Keenan stopped banging on the door, frozen in terror. His breath fogged up the glass and his eyes closed tightly trying to banish the imagery from his mind. And then he felt it. An icy breath on his neck. And he felt a presence. He lifted his head straight and opened his eyes. Staring at him in the window to the basement was his own reflection. And nothing more. He breathed a sigh of relief and turned away from the door.

The pitchfork ripped into his body so quickly, that at first, he didn't even feel it. His mind was still trying to process the fact that he was now several feet up, impaled and the person holding the handle was Nat.

As the initial shock wore away and the pain began searing through his body, he looked down and saw his own blood dripping down the long prongs of the fork. He looked again at Nat. Her eyes were not her own. They were milky, clouded. And surrounded by dark shadows.

With a final thrust, she shoved the fork forward with such force that it went through Keenan's back, and through the metal of the door, pinning him there. As she released the handle, Keenan took his last breath. A small smile crept across her face as she turned and walked away, making her way through the store. She stopped next to one of the two giant Christmas trees near the front of the store. To her left she saw Jodie's illuminated body hanging there. To her right was the mutilated body of Ben, lying under a teddy bear. And turning around, she could see a puddle of blood making its way under the staff doors from Keenan's impaled form. The smile returned briefly, and she vanished from view.

As the last of the snow was shovelled out of the way of the main entrance, the tech support team climbed out of their van, clutching their latte cups and engrossed in their phones. Parked alongside them was the security team that had locked the store up the previous night.

"I'm surprised you guys could get yourselves out of bed on Christmas Eve," one of the guards said sarcastically.

The tech team gave him a cursory glance, and then returned their gaze to their screens, pausing only to take brief sips of coffee.

"Yeah, good talking to you."

"Let's get the damn doors open, Jerry. Sooner we start, the sooner I can get back home to my family. This was supposed to be my day off."

The keys clicked into the locks, and behind them eager customers were already flocking forwards. Turning to give them a look of disgust, bearing in mind it was only seven-thirty in the morning, Jerry addressed them.

"Hey, you guys need to get a life. We don't open until nine!"

Muttered swearing from the crowd echoed around the car park, but the shoppers didn't leave, and instead began queueing up by the main entrance. Unperturbed, security turned their keys, and the shutters began to open. Something did not seem right almost immediately. Jerry and the other guard could see lights inside the store. There shouldn't be any lights on. And then the screams echoed around the entire neighbourhood as the full grizzly sight came into view.

The two Christmas trees at the front of the store were fully illuminated with fairly lights, both clear and multicoloured. But decorating the trees were the bodies of the four youths claimed by the spirits of the store. The lights and their chords wove in and out of their mouths, lighting up their eyes *from behind* and stringing them tightly to the trees themselves. All around the base of the trees was a thick sticky pool of crimson red. Several people ran, terrified whilst others began violently being sick.

Jerry ran to call the police while the other guard was frozen in horror. In the remaining crowd however, who had begun filming and taking pictures of the horrific scene, stood Nat. Her eyes once again glazed over, and that same eerie smile spread across her face.

As the sirens began to come into hearing range up above, down in the basement, beams of daylight were just starting to penetrate through the tiny windows in the far wall. As a single ray of sunlight hit the discarded Nokia 3310, still sitting in the pentagram, the screen on the device came to life, and the phone began to vibrate. On the screen, just visible due to the lack of back light on the device were two words.

'Mum Calling.'

ADDITIONAL CONTENT

CANCELLED

"John, we've been here before. Every time you think you've got a juicy lead for a new investigation, we end up splitting an episode in half, and it just doesn't work."

John, uncharacteristically slammed his hand down on the desk. He was adamant that he was right, and the network executives were wrong. This place… this place was fucking perfect.

"This isn't another split episode I promise you, Hank. This shit is the real deal. I've already got Hector scouting out the local area, and he's getting dozens of witness reports. We have to do this!"

Hank shook his head. He was far from convinced. He had seen the recent viewing figures, suspected controversy surrounding his host, and the board were not thinking about ploughing more money into a sinking ship. A fact he had not yet told John, despite him being an executive producer of his own show.

John Slater was the next Zak Bagans. Or at least, that's what he would tell himself. He collected a crew of five, consisting of co-investigator Hector, and equipment techs Will, Wes and Frank. They had filmed a documentary using just their iPhone cameras ten years earlier, and submitted it to all of the networks from Discovery through to the BBC. The only one to pick it up, however, had been an independent station called True Horror. They had given John a six episode deal, and a modest budget to go out on the road and try and emulate the success that the likes of Ghost Adventures and Most Haunted had developed over the years. The first season had been a roaring success, and as a reward, True Horror had given John and his team a three-season deal, each consisting of ten episodes, and a much improved budget. The problem was, that was ten years ago, and the climate had shifted somewhat.

Whilst the likes of Ghost Adventures continued to rise after nearly 30 seasons, John's show which had been titled 'Shadowlands' had started to decline after season six. True Horror had been purchased by CBS and liquidated so as to not clash with their programming, and Shadowlands had been moved to an 11pm slot on a Sunday night on CBS Reality.

Controversy didn't help either. It was reported after a recent investigation at a toy store, in Wealdstone, that John had gotten into an argument with one of the teenagers working there, who had tried to mess with their equipment. A customer managed to snap a blurry photo which looked as though John punched him across the face. While it was indeed a blurry photo, the press had run with it, and viewership had gone down drastically. Comments found their way across social media such as, 'someone should smack that Bagans wannabe back!' and 'does anybody even watch this dude anymore?'

But this was different. John had taken the team back to Wealdstone to investigate 1701 Pike Road and supposed haunted dolls, when a local had approached the crew and told them they knew of a far more active location. Whilst John had always harboured a secret ambition to investigate the Crossroads settlement on the outskirts, something Zak Bagans had never done, the woman told him about Highland Manor. Instantly, he was fascinated. But Hank decided now was the time to deliver the hammerblow.

"John, the board wants to cancel Shadowlands."

For a moment, John said nothing, and remained perfectly still. After a minute or so, Hank thought he had died from the shock, such was his stillness.

"John?"

When John spoke, it was with such a monotone response, it gave him the illusion that John had morphed into some kind or robot.

"Give me a 2 hour special. One-off. Outside of the regular season. If it tanks, I'll agree to cancellation. But if it's a hit, I want a new deal. 3 seasons, 30 episodes."

Despite the state of the show, Hank really did enjoy it. He found the more amateurish aspects endearing and truthful. And he loved John's passion for his career. But he knew this would be a hard task to convince the board. They wanted to save money, now he was being asked to fund a special episode.

"Leave it with me."

Three days later, post production was in full swing on the 1701 Pike Road episode, which meant John and the team were available for filming once more. And they had been given the green light.

The board had told Hank that they would fund the special, and agree to John's conditions. They even offered to move Shadowlands back to it's previous 9pm slot on Friday nights if the show was indeed a success. In truth though, the executives were convinced it would fail and they would not only manage to get a drain on funds off the books, but also be able to write off the special after completion as a tax write off.

But, here they were, standing outside Highfield Manor, with John standing central at the base of the steps leading up to the house. The camera was trained on him, and he gave his introductory speech.

"Welcome to a Shadowlands 2-hour special. This is not out first visit to Wealdstone, but it promises to be our most active and dangerous location to date. We have had reports of multiple spirits, demons and poltergeist activity to such a level, that our previous investigation in this town was interrupted by locals, warning us of the dangers and begging us to investigate. What else could we do? This is Shadowlands."

"CUT!"

John's shoulders untensed, and he walked quickly down to the cameras, and spoke to Hector who was off to the side, simply staring up at an attic window.

"How was that?" John asked him, but Hector was still distracted. "Hello? Hector?"

Hector snapped out of his daze.

"Sorry dude, what did you say?"

John shook his head.

"Never mind, I'll redo it later. Needs more drama anyway."

As John walked away, Hector's eye was once again caught by a shadow, a black mass moving past the same attic window. He felt like he was being watched, and the sensation garnered a shiver throughout his body. Nevertheless, John broke the moment once again as he shouted for the entire crew to go inside and set up the X-Cameras and other equipment ahead of the first interviews. As Hector walked into the house for the first time, he had no idea that he would never leave.

John had fewer possessions in the CBS offices than he thought. Just a poster on the wall from their first season on True Horror, the usual forms for permit applications and filming requirements, and a photograph of him and the team at their first shoot. He looked at Hector, standing beside him, smiling, arms around his shoulders.

The Highland Manor shoot had been a staggering success. Simply, not in the way John had hoped. Hector had seemingly died of a heart attack days later, but John knew the truth. He'd seen the way Hector had been preoccupied with something upon their arrival, and he knew with his experiences, and the feel of that set that his friend and colleague had never truly left. Hector's death was reported in every media outlet in the US and even crossed the pond. Reporters showed up, paparazzi were everywhere, and the ratings for the show went stratospheric. It gained the highest viewership for a paranormal show in history. But when the deal had been presented to John to sign, guaranteeing his financial and television future, he turned it down.

His preference, was for the show to continue with Will, Wes and

Frank with a new host. He simply didn't feel he could continue on, knowing how he had pushed so hard for the investigation at Highland Manor, only for it to cost the life of his friend. But the network said no. It was John or nothing.

The cancellation came as no surprise to him, but it spent at least 3 weeks in the entertainment news. The crew went their separate ways, blaming him for the collapse of the best thing that had ever happened to them, and now John was essentially blacklisted.

"Hey John."

Hank's voice spoke softly through a crack in the door. He entered and approached John slowly, hands in pockets, shoulders bunched up, visibly uncomfortable.

"Hank."

While John didn't blame him for what had transpired, he had no desire to fraternize with anyone that represented the network right now. He just wanted to collect his things and be gone.

"You got some work?" Hank asked, regretting the question as soon as it left his lips.

John closed his rucksack, and swung it onto his shoulder. He paused, took a deep breath and answered his former boss.

"Got a lead on something weird happening in the Bahamas. Weird storms, sightings of spirits. Gonna go take a look. Severance pay may as well be used on something useful."

Hank stood aside as John moved to walk past him, which he did with such speed, Hank almost fell onto the desk behind him. After John had left, Hank noticed something had been left behind on John's desk. As he leaned to pick it up, he saw it was some kind of key. Having watched the special, he knew it to be the key to the basement of Highland Manor that the spirits apparently liked to move around. He picked up the key, examined it and felt an overwhelming energy coming from the ornate metal design.

There was no answer to Hank's knock on the door of Highland Manor. But something compelled him to try the door. It swung open, with the stereotypical creak in the hinges as it did so.

"Hello?" he called, but nobody answered him.

He made his way into the house and noticed there was now construction happening at various points. As he wandered through the ground floor, he noticed this construction stopped at the door to the basement, for which they key in his pocket belonged. Either side of the door were two new brick walls, and discarded materials beside those. Hank walked up to the door, which, naturally, was locked. He took out the key, turned it in the lock and opened the door.

"Hello?" he cried out once again.

"Hank?" came a reply.

Two steps in, and Hank called out again.

"Hello? Who is that?"

Again, the reply, but this time closer and clearer.

"Hank? Down here."

Ten steps down, and now fully consumed by the darkness, Hank stopped. The voice belonged to a male, early forties, with a distinctive accent. As Hector's face emerged from the darkness, partially transparent, and eyes as black as the darkness surrounding him, Hank clutched his chest as pain seared through him. He desperately tried to turn back the way he came, but above him, the door slammed shut, they key turned in the lock with a click, and the key fell from the door. The pain in Hank's chest worsened, his brow covered in a cold sweat. As a coppery taste entered his mouth, Hector's demonized face was now almost upon him.

"Your turn to be cancelled, Hank."

As John placed the final brick into position, fully covering the basement door, he couldn't help but smile. Hank's cries had long died out, and John was grateful that he had been left to enact his plan. As he walked out the front door and down the path to his car, he smiled to himself.

Once inside the car, he took out a small manilla envelope, and placed the key to the basement inside. He then placed a note that he took out of his inside pocket into the envelope before sealing it up. The address was a Wealdstone one, and the recipient written in bold capital letters above the address.

Kathryn Silverton
Wealdstone Haunted Museum

AFTERWORD

I have, over the years, thanked many people from all aspects and avenues of my life in the backs of my books. Sometimes, even mentioning famous people who have inspired me, despite I knew all too well that they would never see it. But, it was my book and I could say what I wanted to!

Now the series is coming to an end, I would like to unify my acknowledgements across the board into this one message. Particularly as I have even more people to thank years after the first book hit websites!

First and foremost, I must thank my incredible wife, Charlotte. Without her, I simply do not know where I would be, not just with my writing but in my life. I was starting to give up on almost everything when I met her, and she quickly became my rock, my confidante, and more importantly, my best friend. It is with her that I was able to start a family, and in February 2022, we welcomed little Molly Rose Adams into the world. They are both my world, and entire universe and I simply cannot imagine anywhere in the multiverse where we aren't all together.

Naturally, the next in line for thanks and appreciation would be my parents, Shirley and Vince Adams. Particularly since my introduction to various forms of social media in the last few years, I have come across far too many stories of unhappy childhoods, and lack of support from families of many people in my life. I, fortunately, am certainly not one of them. My mother and father have never once put me down, attempted to dissuade me from doing anything or making any significant life changes. They have shown me nothing but unconditional love, support, and at times, financial help. They continue to be a beacon of light in my life, and are devoted to my little family completely. If there was a blueprint on how to parent a child, these two would have written it.

That support flows down the family chain, and emanates from my sister, Francesca too. When we were younger, we did not get on. Always hitting each other, shouting at each other, and making each other unhappy and angry almost every day. But as we have gotten older, our bond has strengthened, and she has been there for me, Charlotte and Molly every step of the way. It has even reached the point where we left our home in Plymouth, and moved to Dorset, just a matter of streets away from each other! Her other half, Anthony, is a tower of strength for her, and their two children Jack and Isabelle are the jewels in their little family. It is a joy to be in their company, and their unique place on the autistic spectrum makes them extra loveable, and always fun to be around, because they adore companionship. I'm proud to be their uncle.

My grandparents played a vital role in my early life. My grandfather, William Henry Griffiths, for whom the first book is dedicated, was my best friend. I would see him every fortnight growing up, and he would always have a happy and yet powerful aura around him. He was a huge imposing figure in stature, but was as kind as could be. There were always miniature bars of chocolate in a tin waiting for me and Francesca, and a couple of quid pocket money. His death in 2005 devastated me, and in truth, 18 years later, still resonates within me. I miss him dearly.

My other grandparents, Marlene and Dave are a force of encouragement and love. Nobody fucks with my Nan. Not if they know what is good for them. I remember distinctly her glaring at my soon to be mother-in-law at our wedding when the registrar spoke the words 'if anyone knows of any reason why these two should not be married, speak now.' It was definitely a 'don't fuck with me' look. And of course my Grandad is nothing but a funny cuddle teddy bear, even now. His humour always cuts through any tension or discomfort, as bad as his jokes are, and I was proud to ask him to be my best man at my wedding, where he made the customary jokes, and I was blessed that he accepted.

I never had a job that I truly loved, until I moved to Ilfracombe in North Devon about a year and a half after my maternal grandfather died. I spent 10 months hunting for a job to no avail, before being told that whole time, the fruit and veg shop next door had been looking for someone! And so in the September of 2008, I began what would turn out to be 8 years working for the Norman family. That family made me feel like one of my own. I owe a debt of gratitude to Pam Norman for being my extra grandmother, Trevor and Sarah Norman for showing me such kindness, support and friendship, and Paula Hobman and her family for being like a crazy aunt and always cheering me up. I miss working for them, and being around them all the time, but they left an everlasting mark on my life that I will always carry with me.

Charlotte's Great Uncle Richard Oliver, and his daughter Nancy, have become two of our strongest connections. They have always backed us with whatever choices we made, and helped us along the way. They exude love and support, and at certain times, I'm not sure what we would have done without them. I simply cannot accurately place into words, what the two of them mean, but I like to think that they know.

And finally, I would like to take a minute or two to mention some of the people I have met in recent years through the wonders of the online community.

I joined Flare in 2023, a peer support group for those dealing with mental health issues and physical disabilities. It is a place to talk together, support others, and build a friendly safe community in the often toxic world of the internet. Founded by Robyn, Josh and Emma, it has gone from strength to strength and in doing so, I gained some very good friends. Like many friends, we have our differences, but the benefit they have given to my life has helped me develop my persona, particularly through their support of my social media presence and helping me to be more outgoing through mentoring and doing my own livestreams. Robyn in particular was instrumental in that, and for someone who has gone through so much in her short life, she gives so much more.

In the same timeframe, I met Chantel. Much like my Nan, you don't fuck with Chantel. She is fierce, devoted and loving in a way that makes her a very treasured individual. I have given her cause to digitally slap me in the face numerous times, but I have never stopped admiring her and the person she has become through the adversity she has battled through. I hope we remain friends for a long time to come.

BookTok's community changed me for the better. I met some wonderful author friends, and not only are they kind and supportive and funny, they are extremely talented writers and designers.

RD Baker is one of my closest author friends. Which is no mean feat considering she lives in Australia! I had never read either a fantasy or spicy book until I was enraptured by her book *Shadow and the Draw*. The world building was so well done and yet I was able to follow it all! I have since joined her ARC team and anticipate every book she writes with rising enthusiasm. She is also an incredible advocate for indie authors, and kindness across the world. If you haven't read her books before, what are you doing with your life?!?!

Next up is someone who I came across during a giveaway she was doing on TikTok. Alexia Mulle-Rushbrook very kindly sent me a free copy of her dystopian sci-fi The Minority Rule, and once I read it, I immediately bought the rest of the trilogy, devouring each book. They were simply wonderful, and I was happy to become part of her ARC team for the more recent release *They Call Me Angel*, which was her best work to date. She is a kind and giving person, and we chat often through direct messages, and always support each other on TikTok.

And no thanks would be complete without the presence of Christian Francis. I came across him when I saw one of his many videos on TikTok offering advice to indie authors like me, and everything the man said made perfect sense, and I followed it often. I particularly enjoyed his video on writing a scary scene which I may have coerced into a particular chapter of *Frame of Mind*, so this is me giving him credit! He also very kindly was the man behind this redesign of *The Dark Corner* series, and I will never forget the time, effort and resources he provided to me for that task. As if that wasn't enough, he designed the covers for my other series *The Frozen Planet Trilogy*, and created the amazing *myindiebookshelf.com* which champions indie authors, giving them a platform to showcase their work and link people exactly where to find them. And let's not forget that his books are fucking awesome. Disturbing… but fucking awesome.

Well, I have rambled on long enough. It's almost as if I was reciting my life story at times, I know, but with this being the best version of my work out there, I wanted to really get the message across.

Arnold Schwarzenegger says often that people are free to call him many things, but don't ever call him a self-made man. Because he has had help from people all his life, and without them, he wouldn't be who he is today. And that sums up perfectly how I feel. Without all the people I mentioned above, I wouldn't be who I am today.

I have written many books since my debut, and I am proud of most of them. While *The Dark Corner* series comes to an end, other journeys begin, and I am happy to say I don't see me stopping typing away anytime soon. So thank you for joining me on the journey, and I hope we can go on many more adventures together as the years go by.

Oh and one more thing…

It is possible to make no mistakes and still lose. That is not failure, that is life. I feel too many people forget that, particularly in this industry.

Take care, and see you in Sisko's.

David W. Adams
November 2023

ABOUT THE AUTHOR

David was born in 1988 in Wolverhampton, England. He spent most of his youth growing up in nearby Telford, where he attended the prestigious Thomas Telford School. However, unsure of which direction he wished his life to go in, he left higher education during sixth form, in order to get a job and pay his way. He has spent most of his life since, working in retail.

In 2007, following the death of his grandfather William Henry Griffiths a couple of years earlier, David's family relocated to the North Devon coastal town of Ilfracombe, where he got a job in local greengrocers, Normans Fruit & Veg as a general assistant, and spent 8 happy years there. In 2014, David met Charlotte, and in 2016, relocated to Plymouth to live with her as she continued her University studies.

In 2018, the pair were married, and currently reside on the Isle of Portland, Dorset.

The first published works of David's, was *The Dark Corner*. It was a compilation of short haunting stories which he wrote to help him escape the reality of the Coronavirus pandemic in early-mid 2020. However, it was not until January 2021, that he made the decision to publish.

From there… *The Dark Corner Literary Universe* was spawned….

You can follow David on TikTok @davidwadams.author.

tiktok.com/@davidwadams.author

amazon.com/stores/author/B08VHD911S

Milton Keynes UK
Ingram Content Group UK Ltd.
UKHW021849250124
436727UK00018B/99/J